DEVIL GIRLS

ED WOOD Jr.

CW00551092

GORSE

GORSE
231 Portobello Road
LONDON W11 1LT
UK

DEVIL GIRLS
ISBN: 1 899006 03 6
Copyright © 1967 by Pad Library
Copyright renewed 1995 by Kathleen O'Hara Wood

British Library Cataloguing in Publication Data.
A catalogue record for this book is available from The British Library.

Cover design by Jane Walker

Printed and bound by The Guernsey Press Co. Ltd., Guernsey.

BOOKS AVAILABLE FROM

GORSE

THE GOSPEL SINGER - HARRY CREWS - £8.99
CLASSIC CREWS - HARRY CREWS - £9.99
LET ME DIE IN DRAG - ED WOOD JR - £5.99
DEVIL GIRLS - ED WOOD JR - £5.99

ALSO AVAILABLE ON COMPACT DISC

DORA SUAREZ - DEREK RAYMOND, JAMES JOHNSTON, TERRY EDWARDS - £10.00
THE WORST! (AN ED WOOD JR MUSICAL) - JOSH ALAN FRIEDMAN - £10.00

FORTHCOMING TITLES

THE MULCHING OF AMERICA - HARRY CREWS
KARATE IS A THING OF THE SPIRIT - HARRY CREWS
A FEAST OF SNAKES - HARRY CREWS
HELL CHICKS - ED WOOD JR
DRAG TRADE - ED WOOD JR
ECRITS DE LAURE - COLETTE PEIGNOT

TO ORDER, OR FOR FURTHER INFORMATION, CONTACT

GORSE

231 PORTOBELLO ROAD LONDON W11 1LT UK
tel-0171 792 9791 fax-0171 792 9871
e.mail-cox @ ballgag.demon.co.uk

UK POSTAGE RATES
BOOKS, ADD £1.50
CDS, POST PAID
FOREIGN RATES, PLEASE ENQUIRE

Introduction

It's hard to recall, as I write this, a time when the name Edward D. Wood Jnr didn't spring readily to the lips, but it's only over the last ten years that Ed, or more correctly, his films, have been dusted off, reviewed, reviled, and then reassessed as genuinely entertaining and surprisingly interesting pieces of work. Of course, the fact that Ed liked to hang around in tight pencil skirts, angora sweaters and long blonde wigs hasn't hurt any in winning him a little extra posthumous publicity, but then, when it comes down to it, you can't really separate the man from his films. Or indeed, as you are about to find out, from his books.

The recently released Tim Burton movie starring Johnny Depp has done a lot to focus attention on one of the forgotten men of cinema, but although the line walked in that film was that Ed's work should be appreciated and enjoyed for what it is - a flawed but delight-filled labour of love and enthusiasm - the reappraisal started in a far less generous way. I guess the Medved brothers have a lot to answer for. When these smart young film critics launched their Golden Turkey awards, Ed was right up there in the number one spot - *Plan 9 From Outer Space* was, by their standards, THE definitive movie turkey. This one just about had it all, and then some. Cheap and shoddy sets. Cheaper and shoddier special effects. Off-kilter acting - some bad, some merely indifferent. Weirdos. Second-rate writing. And a brief appearance by that old ham Bela Lugosi, now officially a movieland joke thanks to his overly stylised technique and gloomy one-note presence. Oh yeah, those Medved boys must have felt pretty comfy and safe when it came to nominating *Plan 9* for the top spot. No one could actually find something to like in this piece of crud, right? Completely and utterly wrong, my little Medved chums, we can now chorus with immense and smug satisfaction.

Rather than consigning *Plan 9* and its maker to the celluloid dumpster, what the Medveds actually achieved was the complete opposite. Sure, we came to laugh, but lingered for a second look. Then a third, then a fourth, and maybe a few more.

Plan 9 seems increasingly, in these days of mind-bogglingly convincing SFX, to embody the appeal of fantastic film making in its youth, and the desire to create a world of wonder overruling the common sense dreariness that prevails when folks start pointing out that the spacecrafts are really paper plates and that none of the actors can act. And of course, once you've been piqued by *Plan 9*, you inevitably make your way to Ed's masterpiece - *Glen Or Glenda*. See, even though the basic premise - closet transvestite makes low-budget movie about closet transvestite and plays the lead role - even though it sounds on paper like a mildly amusing (for all the wrong reasons) journey into Hacksville, the film kind of stays with you. *Glen Or Glenda* makes you laugh but unlike say, *Tango And Cash* or *Bird On A Wire*, or even Kazan's *The Arrangement* or Kubrick's *Full Metal Jacket*, it isn't forgotten completely and utterly the very next morning.

Nowadays of course, Ed no longer suffers from the 'worst director' tag. It gets dragged up (no pun intended) occasionally, but in this weird end-of-the-millenium pop culture stew we all swim around in, words like 'good'and 'bad' no longer count for much: we can pretty much enjoy anything we fancy. ABBA are as hip as Nirvana, you can wear your trousers as flared or as tight around the ankle as you wish, and no one would blink an eye if you said that you think Glen Or Glenda is one of the ten best movies ever made. We live in a Burger King society - whichever way you want it, well, you got it.

One thing I find weird about the whole Wood phenomenon is that on the surface at least, the films aren't actually that much odder or shoddier than many other shoestring efforts released about the same time. So why is it that *Zontar, The Thing From Venus* or *Killers From Space* have escaped both the derision and admiration currently attracted by Wood's movies? They too feature laughable premises and 'variable' acting, yet are forgotten, whereas Ed ... well, I'm writing and you're reading about him right now. It must come down to the man himself.

If you're a cynical type you may conclude that it was his feeble and rather sad regurgitation of already tired bargain basement sci-fi cliches that make his films so extreme. If like me, however, you're an optimistic woolly-headed old pussycat, you will insist that his sheer love of movies and stars and fantasy and life itself shines right through every single badly composed frame of every one of his half-baked flicks. In return, you just have to love them.

Which is why, in certain circles, the long-awaited publication of Ed's novels will be greeted with much the same joy as the discovery of an unpublished Dickens manuscript might be amongst more conventionally academic quarters. At last we get the chance to sample the great one's tortured mind unleashed and unfettered - no longer bound by who and what he could throw together for his cinematic escapades. This promises to be pure Ed of the 100% unrefined bootleg hooch variety, churned out, if Wood historians are to be believed, on a battered old portable in a tiny flea-bag apartment on Hollywood Blvd for whatever meagre coinage was on offer from the cheap-bastard mob-connected porno publishers of the late sixties and early seventies, God Bless 'em. But does it stand up to the movie stuff ? Is it as 'good' or 'bad' as *Jailbait* or *I Married A Monster* ?

A brief dip into the opening chapter of *Let Me Die In Drag*, in which Glen/Glenda makes a welcome return, will have any Ed Wood fan smiling broadly in anticipation of the pleasures to come - out and out sleaze, but with that unique personal touch. The style is pretty much classic Ed: terse, basic, straightforward but very, very strange. Who else would bother writing that the sound of a flushing toilet prevented someone from hearing part of a conversation? Where else would you find a fight breaking out between a transvestite and a hoodlum over the rough treatment of a sweater ? The answer, my friends, is no one; the answer, you lucky dogs, is right here.

Which is why, if you like Ed's films or you like pulp fiction of the cheesier type; if you like transvestites or you like to carry around paperbacks which actually scream "whoever reads me is hip, hip, hip!"; or if you just find yourself hopelessly drawn to the bittersweet poignancy of the starving, derided, tortured but eternally optimistic artist that was Ed D. Wood Jnr, these books deserve to be read.

Ed, we've missed you. Welcome back.

Jonathan Ross, London 1995

CHAPTER ONE

Sheriff Buck Rhodes sat cross-legged, smoking a cigarette in the open right-hand door of his patrol car. It was his third cigarette in the twenty minutes he had been sitting there, but he hadn't realized that fact. His eyes were hypnotically fastened on the great, black expanse of the Gulf of Mexico which sprawled out in front of him. He knew somewhere out there a ship was carefully propelling its way toward the Texas coastline, perhaps even to one of the many moorings at the edge of his own town. A ship which should have been flying the death-head and crossbones of the pirate from its mast head. But the death-head and crossbones would not be representing pirate activities. Rather, it would stand for the cargo of death the ship carried. *Heroin and marijuana from deep along the Mexican coastline,* the rumble had it. And his town was numbered among the smaller, less patrolled ones which situated itself along the water's edge.

There were a hundred or more places along the immediate coastline where a small boat could be hidden without fear of detection. Even the moorings, right out in the open, were comparatively safe. How many search warrants would it take, and how many men, to board every boat coming into and going out of the area? How could he hope to have any real success in such an operation when there was only a force of himself and four deputies?

Buck shook his head hopelessly and stretched a foot over to crush his cigarette out on the ground as he thought back over the past two nights. His informant had been a lovely young school teacher, Harriett Long, who had overheard the information while she was being raped and fatally mutilated by a gang of sadistic juvenile delinquents. She died in the hospital before she could identify her assailants or give any more information about the expected drop. Two full days of questioning suspected juveniles had led him exactly nowhere, except to that lonely spot on the docks, watching the calm, dark waters.

"Where and when will it happen?" he said aloud, then cursed under his breath as he snaked across the seat and got behind the wheel. He started the motor and jerked the car forward so that the right hand door snapped shut by itself. "The teacher is dead and I haven't got a lead. What the hell can I do about it?" he shouted to the deserted road ahead, then snapped on the siren for no other reason than he wanted to annoy someone as his thoughts were annoying him.

Teacher Harriett Long was dead but her memory was still very strong in the minds of the three teenage girls who concealed themselves across from the house she had shared with her sister. Each wore tight-fitting sweaters, Levi's and dirty white sneakers which could cause any move to be as silent as a cat's tread. They were Dee, Babs and Rhoda, three members of a disreputable girl gang known as THE CHICKS. Their eyes searched both ways on the deserted street which surrounded a new model station wagon parked in front of the house. It was a long moment of studied silence before any of them spoke, and when they finally did speak it was in controlled whispers.

"You sure that's the right set of bolts?" Dee, the leader, spoke as she turned to Babs, the girl on her left.

"Sure. I double-checked it. The skinny sister is drivin' it now, but it was teacher's." Babs was a bit annoyed at being doubted, but she dared not defy her leader. Dee was tough when she was defied. She had left a good number of broken noses and split lips in the wake of her rise to power, and at the present there wasn't one girl in the gang who would attempt to question her authority.

Rhoda Purdue, the third member of the party and by far the prettiest, leaned in close to Dee.

"What's the reason?"

"To burn the sonofabitchin' car, what else?" snapped Dee.

"But why? The teacher bitch is dead! What good's it going to do to burn her car now? We can't hurt her anymore." Rhoda was honestly puzzled.

It became immediately apparent Dee would have nothing she did questioned. "Maybe for kicks," she snapped more vehemently. "Look! Bluenose caused us ALL a lot of trouble. The boys knew how to take care of her, so now it's up to us to see they all remember and keep remem-

9

bering, we don't stop just because they're in the grave. Nobody turns any of us in to the fuzz for any reason and gets away with it. We do our job and the boys do theirs. And we got a lot to do to catch up with the boys on this one... they did her up but brown..."

"They sure did," giggled Babs. "Probably the only piece of tail she ever got in her whole life. Oh boy, what a jazzin' she got! Jazzed her right outta' this world." Her eyes went wide in the ecstasy of exciting memories. "Man oh man, did she scream!"

The sound of an automobile motor interrupted Bab's words, and the three girls ducked down into the thicker mesquite brush along the roadside. When the car stopped on the road near their position without cutting the motor off, Dee risked a look toward it. Immediately she snapped back and let the protection of the brush fold around her again. "It's that cop sheriff," she whispered, then she lay flat on the ground and with extreme caution parted some of the lower branches. Her keen eyes glowered as she watched Sheriff Rhodes light a cigarette and look to the house across from them for a long moment. Finally he once more put the car into gear and drove off.

Dee stood up and watched the car until it was gone from sight. "He's gone. Okay! Let's get at it and make it quick!"

Rhoda and Babs stood up, this time both of them held five-gallon cans of gasoline in their hands. In one quick move they raced across the street to the parked station wagon. Dee stood several steps away while both Babs and Rhoda sloshed gasoline over both the exterior and the interior of the vehicle. Then when Rhoda's can was nearly empty, Dee stepped in to take it from her hand. She started a long, thin line of the spilled fluid at the rear of the car and trailed it back some hundred yards or more along the road and there stopped. Babs emptied the remainder of her container into the inside of the car then raced along the road to join Dee and Rhoda.

"You got the other can?" asked Dee.

Babs lifted the container. "Right with me."

"We don't want no fingerprints left behind."

Then Dee leaned over the thin line of gasoline at her feet, studied it briefly, then lit a match and touched the explosive mixture off.

The fire sped along the thin line until it hit the main pool under the car. The vehicle exploded as if in one giant sheet of flame.

"Get out of here," ordered Dee. "That cop ain't so far away he didn't hear that blast." And they raced off into the darkness.

There had been no reason for Buck to take that road past Harriett Long's former home. But there had been something he couldn't explain which drew him in that direction... a something which was all powerful enough to control his mind.

When he was abreast of the house all looked serene, the station wagon parked for the night in its usual place. There was a light in an upstairs window denoting Harriett's sister, Millie, had returned from the funeral home and was preparing for bed. All certainly looked well enough.

He lit a cigarette, then drove off. But a mile or so down the road that same overpowering feeling of something amiss hit him again. When the explosion slammed the airwaves, Buck's stomach sank. He knew immediately where the sound originated. He spun the car around and hit the siren in the same move.

Millie raced to the window within seconds of the explosion which shattered several of her windows. At first glance it appeared to her the whole street was on fire. The glare momentarily imbedded on her vision three dark shapes, some distance away, and running swiftly into the deeper blackness. The incident was but a fleeting moment, but a lasting one for Millie. Buck's siren, growing steadily closer, invaded her ears as she turned to put on a robe over her simple nightgown.

Buck burned rubber when he jammed on his brakes a safe distance from the blazing inferno. Millie raced across her lawn and met him at precisely the same moment.

"There were three of them." Millie was near hysteria. "I saw them off there!" she pointed. "In the dark."

Buck looked off. He knew, like rabbits on the plains, they would be gone, swallowed up by the desert brush and the night. "Did you get a look at them?"

"Three young boys."

"Reckon as how you did get a good look at them?"

"Only the three dark figures running off there." She pointed again.

"How do you know they were boys?"

"I could see they were wearing pants. They ran like boys."

Another siren burst into being in the distance.

"I radioed for the fire truck." He sighed and moved in as close to the flames as the heat would permit.

He turned to survey the acres of dark, homeless desert land on all sides of the Long home. Had Millie not been home, or he passing, the fire could well have spread like wild fire across the desert, destroying the house and anything else in its path before it was discovered. The next closest house was more than five miles back along the road toward town, and no fire hydrant water supplies in between.

Buck was thus engrossed as the fire truck with its self-contained water tank drew into position. The chief of the four man crew went immediately to Buck while his men jumped into action with the equipment.

"Know what started it, Buck?"

"Reckon that's something you'll have to tell me, Herb," said Buck through tight lips.

And while the firemen worked feverishly to quench the flames yet another incident was taking place. The shadowy figure of a teenage boy moved cautiously up to a schoolhouse window.

He took a tire iron from his belt and broke the window, then reached up and unlocked it. He looked around to make sure no one had witnessed his actions, then shoved the window open. When this was done he looked back into the darkness and gave a low whistle which caused two more boys of about his own age to materialize from the darkness and walk in to join him. "You first Danny, then Rick."

"Okay, Lonnie," whispered Danny, the first boy, and he hoisted himself up over the window-sill and into the building.

"Get going Rick, and watch the glass. I had to break the window."

"Sure, Lonnie." The second boy hoisted himself up in the same manner and disappeared into the school room.

Once more the third boy, Lonnie, looked cautiously around him, then gripped the window-sill and made his way in to join the others.

The school room they had entered was much the same as any school room the country over, with the exception that since it was a small town school, the desks were a bit more crowded together. In the front of the class was a long blackboard which showed many years of continuous use and the teacher's desk, which was situated in front of it and to the right of the American flag.

Lonnie moved to the teacher's desk quickly and with a sweep of his arm he knocked everything that was there to the floor: books, papers, blotter, a beautiful pen set and a glass of water containing one single rose. "Get to it," he said harshly.

The boys jumped into action immediately, both taking short hatchets from their belts. They tore into the desks leaving a shamble of splintered wood and the metal frames. Lonnie hit the blackboard in several places with his tire iron, then he moved across the room to smash the several windows. Meanwhile Danny ran to the teacher's desk and slammed his hatchet into it with all his might. The fragile wood broke and splintered with each blow, and each blow contained all the venom Danny felt. Rick finished the last of the smaller desks, then raced in beside Danny. He let his hatchet fall once to a leg of the desk; then his eyes caught on something more interesting to him. He raced to the American flag and hoisted it out of its standard. He raised it over his head and there froze.

"Don't touch that flag!" Lonnie's voice was harsh.

"What's eatin' you?" snapped Rick, and Danny stopped his desk wrecking to look across to them.

"I said, don't touch that flag."

Danny stepped in beside Lonnie. "Thought we got the idea to wreck this joint but good?"

"Don't give me any arguments. Just put it back like I said." The fire of anger could be seen in Lonnie's eyes even in that darkness.

Rick shrugged, and silently returned the flag to its standard. "What's that all about, Lonnie?" he asked as he turned back.

15

"I don't like hurtin' the flag. I never did. So that's all I gotta say about it."

The siren of the deputy sheriff's car coming in fast from the distance caused them to snap around. "Get out of here."

Almost as one, the three young men went out through the window and raced across the playground to where their car, a stripped down hot rod, was hidden. They piled in with Lonnie at the wheel, and the twin pipes roared into life. The jalopy raced back across the playground and onto the grass lawn in front of the school to sideswipe the police car just as it turned in toward the school driveway. Before the sheriff's car could be turned around by the deputy at the wheel, the hot rod had already disappeared into the darkness of the night and moments later even the blast of its twin pipes could no longer be heard.

CHAPTER TWO

The three girls, short of breath from their long run, came out of the desert and secreted themselves for a long time in one of the many alleys which led from the unsavory part of town… a section of town made up of beer bars, hamburger joints and, at the far end near the coast, a red-light district. They took deep breaths into painful lungs, and each breath seared their insides until they no longer had to fight to get the air down. Still gasping for breath, Babs said. "Man oh man! Did you see that thing go? Never expected it to blow that way. The skinny bitch must have had a full tank of gas in the rear end. Man oh man! Too bad the skinny bitch wasn't in it." She made a gesture with her hands. "Pow! All gone, skinny bitch!"

Dee and Rhoda didn't answer her remark, figuring there just wasn't anything to answer. And after a long time, and when they were once more breathing easier, the girls made their way through the alley and drifted off with other strollers on the low-class lower part of the main street.

Dee was heading them for the dock area.

"What are we going this way for, Dee?" Rhoda actually didn't like the dock area and kept away from it as much as possible. The red-light district, where they were heading, was a row of houses just before the docks began. And Rhoda knew they were illegal and sooner or later Sheriff Rhodes and his men would knock them over.

Rhoda didn't plan on being around when that happened. The sheriff had knocked them over twice on raids, but hadn't found anything to close them up or convict anybody. But everybody in town knew what went on in those cockroach-infested screw dens... it was only a matter of time. Rhoda knew she had done just about everything the broads in those shacks had done, but in secret, and she liked what she did enough to not want the law finding out. If they ever did they'd put her away and it would be a long time before she could have fun with the boys.

She couldn't stand that. When she wanted a boy, she wanted a boy, and right now. There wasn't any two ways about it. One of the boys was always calling her a Nymphomaniac. She liked the nymph part alright, it sounded nice. But the MANIAC... that she didn't like. She knew what a maniac was and she didn't like to be referred to as such. How could she be a maniac just because she liked to pull her skirt up and her panties down then go to bed with some boy? There was too much fun in it to have anything to do with being a maniac. "Why don't we beat it over to Jockey's Place, pick up a couple of the boys? Maybe they got some stuff and we can get whacked out. The night's young enough for a long, long trip into dreamland."

"Dee's looking for somebody," informed Babs. Rhoda took a cigarette package from the belt-line of her tight Levi's, and a pack of matches from the pocket. She lit up and replaced the pack and matches. "Anybody in particular?"

"It figures. I don't walk around all night just for the fun of it." Her eyes trawled the dark streets ahead.

"Oh man, our leader talks so much," mused Babs.

"If I wanted you to know any more I'd told you before."

"That's right Dee. You sure ain't one for words. But I don't like mysteries. Not even on television." Babs took the cigarette from Rhoda's mouth, took a deep puff, then replaced it between the pretty girl's lips. "Not even on television," she repeated.

"He ain't no mystery."

"Now at least we know we're lookin' for a HE," shrugged Babs.

"The kind that comes down here I need like a hole in the head," rejected Rhoda.

"You'd take any kind that came along when you need it, just like your pot." She stopped as a movement further along the street caused her to halt her words before they had finished. She snapped her gaze toward the direction of the intruder. Her eyes narrowed as they tried to pierce the darkness. Then recognition directed her tones. "It's Holy Joe!"

"How can you tell?" Rhoda shivered suddenly.

"Nobody else walks like that. Like he's always going to meetin'."

"What do you suppose he's doin' down here?" Rhoda stepped a bit more into the shadows.

"One of two things," grinned Dee. "Savin' souls or gettin' laid."

Rhoda didn't think the remark so funny. "We better blow!"

Dee took hold of her arm, and her fingers pressed tightly into the sweater-covered flesh.

"I'll tell you when to blow." She let go of the girl's arm in a snapping motion which spun her toward a brick wall, then she also moved to the wall and leaned up against it. Bab's followed the lead.

"Damn," said Rhoda. "He's in thick with my old lady." She tossed her cigarette to the ground and crushed it out with the toe of her low-heeled shoe.

"I oughta make you pick that up and eat it," Dee sneered, flashing her angry eyes from the snuffed out cigarette butt up to Rhoda's eyes. But the clergyman was getting too close for any more words. "We'll talk more about that later." Her tone meant what she said.

Reverend Steele was a man in his early thirties with one distinguishing mark, other than his handsome features. He had a shock of white-grey along the middle of his otherwise full head of wavy, dark hair. He wore the round, white collar in pride and determination of purpose. In himself he had, however, a great insight for the problems of others. When he had graduated the seminary, he was given a choice of congregations anywhere in the world. Without a second thought Reverend Steele picked his own hometown. He knew the people, young and old, good and bad. And he knew the problems which needed solving. He felt with all his heart he could do his best work there in Almanac, Texas.

Reverend Steele put on his best smile and tipped his black felt hat. "Good evening, young ladies," he said.

Dee and Babs looked to each other, then away along the street. Reverend Steele turned his smiling face full on Rhoda. "We've missed you at the church club lately, Rhoda..."

"Now ain't that an original line," snapped Rhoda, conscious of Dee's menacing eyes on her. "Look, preacher. Go peddle your sewing circles to somebody who needs it. I need it like a hole in the head."

Undisturbed by the girl's remark and tone Reverend Steele retaliated with, "If you'd come, Rhoda, I think you'd find more things to do at the club than sewing..."

Dee jammed her face in close to the man. "You ain't sellin' us. We like things just the way they are—so now BEAT IT!" Her voice became more intense. "What in hell you doin' down here in the red-light district anyway?"

"Looking for HELL," he said simply; then as he turned, he threw a parting shot at Rhoda. "We'll see you soon, Rhoda."

"No you won't," shouted Dee. "Now lay offa' her!"

"Good evening, girls," the Reverend said and walked again on his way along the street, back toward the bright lights of the main street.

"You played him pretty heavy, Dee," said Rhoda, lighting up another cigarette.

"The holy smucher had it comin'. Down here he's damned well in my backyard and he plays the way I want him to play. He don't like it he can damned well get the hell out. I don't hafta talk with him." Her anger again boiled over at Rhoda. "You keep backin' down in front of that bastard and I'll give you a goin' over you won't never see matched in your whole life."

"Ahh, lay off me," frowned Rhoda.

Dee was about to continue when a door in the house next to the brick wall opened. A man's voice came from within the dark interior. "Dee! Over here, Dee!"

Dee spun toward the sound then motioned for the other girls to follow her as she made her way to the opening just as a sharply-dressed young man stepped out to meet them. Directly behind him one of the house girls in a sheer negligee lazied up against a dirty hall siding. She watched the action through half-lids, through narcotic-glazed eyes, but said nothing. "I waited until the deity went on his way," said the young man, then smiled. "Good to see you again, Dee."

Babs crept up beside Dee, her eyes all aglow. "So he's the big mystery. Come to think of it Lark, you are a mystery."

"Makes me all the more alluring, baby."

"Shut up," commanded Dee of her girls before she turned her full attention back to Lark.

22

"Lonnie got your message to me."

"Good boy, Lonnie."

"Where ya been keepin' yerself since the last time, Lark? Must be a month or more."

"More! I had a little ocean voyage, down lower Mexico way for a while."

"Something big?"

"Big enough. Blow, girls," he said to Rhoda and Babs.

"Say. How come? We get all the way…" Dee pushed Babs back violently before she could finish her words.

"When Lark says you blow… you blow. Now I'm telling you to blow. So blow!"

"I don't like bein' pushed around." Babs took a step back toward Dee.

"Maybe you'd like a cracked lip?" Her hands were hard on her hips and her eyes were narrow. A narrowness all the girls knew meant trouble. If she were pushed any further.

Babs stopped in her tracks. She glared at Dee another long moment, then turned and started back along the sidewalk toward town. "Jockey's later?" asked Rhoda.

"Yeah. Later."

Rhoda turned and hurried to catch up with Babs, then Dee once more looked to Lark who turned and slammed the door in the half-naked whore's face before he looked to Dee again. A bright smile cracked his features and his hand reached out to mould Dee's ample left breast.

"Just as full as ever, baby," he said in a tenderness which was hard for him to muster.

Dee pulled the sweater up around her neck. She had on no brassiere. "Take a look for yourself. Better'n them creeps in the house behind you any day."

"Honey, you don't have to prove that to me."

"Then why do you go in there all the time."

"If I have to explain, which I don't, it's my hideout."

"That's all?"

"That's all I'm tellin' you about it."

She lowered the sweater and smoothed it over the top of her Levi's again. "You didn't call me all the way down here to admire my tits!"

"That's right, baby. I said it's something big. How good are your girls?"

"Good. Real good. They have to be, to be around me."

"I get you. Any on the stuff?"

"A couple. They're my best girls. They work harder because they need more scratch, to keep their habit healthy."

"I don't want anybody that ain't on the stuff. You can't trust them."

"You want junkies?"

"Now you don't classify yourself as a junkie, do you?"

"Ahh, I can take it or leave it alone,"

"Sure you can." His outspoken words belied known facts inside. "That's why you can be trusted. Like right now. You look a little nervous. Like you might need a fix just to pick you up."

She bit her lip. "Yeah. Yeah, that would be nice. Me and the girls were going over to Jockey's Place and grab a couple of the boys for some gold. I ain't got the scratch to buy any. Would you...?"

"Sure, baby. You're doing me a favor. I'm doing you one. I ain't with the stuff in my pocket, but one of the girls inside will have some."

"I don't like those creepy whores. You know what they do to me everytime I go in there."

"Well now, let's put it this way. They're nice to you, you have to be nice to them. They've never hurt you any, have they?"

"They..."

Lark cut in with his giant smile. "Spare me the details. I've watched enough of your sessions with them. But if you want the stuff from them, that's the way you get it."

She fought back the fever which had slowly been taking her body over the past hour since the fire. She wanted to shoot up, but a session with the whores was a rough way of getting it. She fought back the fever. "What's your big deal?"

"I need your girls. All of them."

"What for?"

"A party Friday night."

"Gimme a fix and you get them."

"I told you how to get your fix."

"You get me one and you get my girls."

"Then, I find another way." He started to turn away.

25

Panic seized the girl. "No! No! Wait." She calmed herself as he turned back to her. "What's in it for me?"

"Five pound brick of mary... you do with it the way you want. Sell it. Use it. Cut it with your girls. Anything you want."

"That much, huh?"

"That much!"

"But I need the white stuff. Mary ain't no good for me."

"Like I said, baby. That's your end. Sell it and you buy your own stuff..."

"Yeah... yeah... that's the way. What have you got?"

"I said it was big. Our little town has become the transfer point from the Mexico outlet to the big boys in the North. I'm the boat man, honey-baby... the boat man. And I gotta get it ashore."

"You got it this far. Why not just row it ashore?"

"Boy, you can be dumb sometimes, Chick... the heat's on all up and down the coast. That teacher you folks put under the ground has every sea port on the watch." He watched her puzzled look as she glanced to him when he men-tionedthe teacher. "Oh yes," he informed. "I heard about your little schoolmarm and her sudden demise. Now, not that I blame you. She got what I suspect was coming to her. But it makes the cheeze more binding as the saying goes. Which makes me figure on a safe angle to get my wares ashore."

"A lot of stuff?"

"Plenty."

"What?"

"Marijuana. Pills. H. L.S.D. The works."

"L.S.D.?" Dee was truly puzzled. "What in hell's that?"

"Lysergic acid diethylamide. If that tells you anything."

"Nothing."

"See. There's no use explaining. Tell you what. If you're a good girl, I'll turn you on sometime before Friday. I took my first trip on the boat, coming here. Wow! What a trip! I was five miles above the boat during the whole experience. I'll turn you on sometime soon."

The talk of his trip into narcotic dreamland excited Dee's imagination to a point of release and her urine drained through her panties and left a wet spot on the front of her Levi's, the remainder ran down her leg... she crossed her legs in anticipation. There was no doubt she would blast off and the whores would do the things they wanted to do with her which they could not fully accomplish with men. "My... my girls will... will do what I say..." she stuttered through dry lips. "What do they do?"

"There's going to be a party. A nice soda pop and milkshake party for the girls on board my boat. Who would expect a bunch of teenage girls—only girls—are bringing ashore a fortune in fly high medicine?"

"Hey, that's pretty slick."

He beamed with pride. "Sure. Your broads go in with size thirty-two brassieres and come out with thirty-eights..."

"And wait until you see the new hip pads and ass pads."

"All the more they can carry. Say, you've been improving your lot since I was here last."

She tried to smile but the craving for heroin made her face feel as if it were cracking. Her hands shook noticably as she stuck her thumbs into the top of her Levi's, trying to push them hard against her belly to keep the nausea she knew would soon be coming from presenting itself. "Meantime, keep out of trouble. Lay off any of your other activities..." she heard him say and she wished he would shut up. Couldn't he tell she was sick? She needed help, not talk. The son of a bitch keeps on talking and talking, always talking. Why don't he shut up?

She snapped to him with the glazed eyes which demanded immediate action. "Now, Lark. Now. Goddamn it, now! You got my girls. You got me. We'll get your stuff. Now, damn it, get me the stuff now... I'll do what ever those whore bitches want. I'll kiss 'em. They can kiss me. They can screw me, they can jazz me. They can whip me. I'll take the high heels in my back, my stomach. I'll take the whip... the paddle. They can kiss my ass for all I care. Just get me a fix. Get me a fix before I die right here on the sidewalk."

He put his arm almost fatherly about her shoulders. "Now we can't let that happen, can we?

28

I wouldn't want to see you dead on the sidewalk. I need my little Dee-Dee too much." He propelled her lightly toward the door he had previously came from. "Come on, the girls will make you well again. In a minute or two you'll be flying over the city. You'll like that, won't you? And all the time you're flying, the girls will be getting their kicks too—now won't they?"

"Oh yes… yes… yes…" Her voice was deep in ecstacy… her mind was racing ahead to the excitement presented to her. He opened the door and she saw the same glaze-eyed whore.

"She's all yours Gloria," Lark said, and the girl with a stone-like glare moved to the doorway and slapped Dee's face, then put her arm around her shoulders and led her off into the darkness of the hall.

CHAPTER THREE

Ruggedly handsome Sheriff Buck Rhodes raced his police car toward the well-lighted two-storey school building. He screeched his brakes on the gravel in front of the main entrance and behind one of his deputy's cars and a black sedan he knew belonged to school principal, Hal Carter. The sheriff wasted no time in mounting the several stone steps and threw open the big doors. Just on the inside he was met by his deputy.

"Where are they Bob?"

"Room nine."

"Who's there?"

"Reverend Steele, Hal Carter and the teacher taught in the wrecked room. June O'Hara..."

"I don't know her."

"She's new on the job. Took over the job of the dead teacher yesterday morning. They flew her in from Houston."

Buck let the information sink in a moment before he spoke again. "Okay, Bob. I'll take over now. You better get back on patrol. No telling what else might happen tonight the way things are going already."

"Right," said the deputy, and moved quickly toward the front doors.

The Sheriff's footsteps made hollow, echoing sounds on the marble-like floor of the empty corridor as he searched out room nine and entered. Both men he knew well, but he had not expected the extra sight he saw. She was a young woman of perhaps twenty five and very beautiful. She wore a fluffy pink angora sweater and a soft brown skirt. He tipped his hat. But before he could speak, Hal Carter, a balding man in his early fifties, stepped up beside them. "Miss O'Hara this is Sheriff Buck Rhodes. Our law enforcement in Almanac."

She extended her hand and tried for a smile, but it was a troubled smile. "It is nice to know you Sheriff Rhodes, even if we do meet under such drastic circumstances."

"Ma'am," he said, lacking other words. Then turned to survey the wrecked room. "They sure made a mess out of this place, didn't they?"

"Vandals," said Mr. Carter and made it sound like a full curse. "The taxpayers will certainly put up a howl about this."

Buck sighed. "Try and tell them what to do about it, and you'll hear them howl even harder."

Miss O'Hara spoke softly. "What can be done Sheriff?"

"I'll tell you what can be done," cut in Carter. "Sheriff, get your men out and pick up every occupant in every hot rod and every hamburger joint on the street. That's what to do."

Reverend Steele stepped into the group. "Come now, Mr. Carter. They aren't all to blame."

Carter spun on the clergyman. "You condone these horrid actions, Reverend Steele?"

"Of course not. But you can't condemn them all for the actions of a few."

"Well I say there are just a few too many. Lock every one of them up and you know the right ones are there."

Miss O'Hara spoke softly, but there was no smile on her face. "In early Chinese law there was such an Emperor as you would have the sheriff be. If there was one murder and he had eight suspects, he ordered all of their heads to be cut off. He also knew in that way he had the right one. Is that the way you would have it, Mr. Carter?"

Mr. Carter mumbled something under his breath then angrily turned to glare out of the window. Sheriff Rhodes directed, then, his full attention on the girl. "I understand you teach this particular classroom Miss O'Hara?"

"Yes. This is a class in Ancient History."

"I see. Thus the Chinese puzzle," he grinned broadly and her smile came up to match his.

"Yes. That and old Charlie Chan movies."

"I preferred the Mr. Moto series."

"You would. He was the more physical type," and she laughed showing a perfect row of white teeth outlined by her rouge-red lips. Her eyes sparkled brightly.

"Miss O'Hara. You are a mighty lovely woman when you smile."

"Well, thank you Sheriff Rhodes."

Carter spun on them. "What in blazes is this— a social in Lovers' Lane?"

Buck did not look to the man. He kept his smiling eyes on those of the girl. "We have one of those here too. Only it looks out over the desert instead of a moonlit lake." He drifted his eyes toward the Reverend and winked before he looked back to Miss O'Hara. "Any of the kids in particular give you a special kind of trouble since you've been here?"

"No more than usual I'm told. I'm afraid the boys in this class aren't quite what one would expect to find at a Sunday school picnic." She let her eyes drift toward those of Reverend Steele, thinking perhaps she had phrased her explanation into a sore spot.

Mr. Carter cut in, breaking the spell. "As Principal of this school, I can say that goes for the girls also. Their short skirts and tight sweaters. Marijuana parties. The girls are just as bad as the boys."

Buck kept his eyes on the girl. "You knew that Miss Long was murdered?"

"I heard."

"Do you know why?"

"There have been rumors."

"Then let me put the rumors straight." Buck talked in light, even tones. He had no intentions of shocking the girl, only telling her what she was in for. "Miss Long was attacked by juveniles. She was murdered because she learned about a shipment of dope coming in by water. But it would seem they are not satisfied with just putting her in her grave. Tonight her automobile was burned, and..." he let his arm sweep the room slowly, "her former school room has been wrecked. You, in taking her place, may be putting yourself in jeopardy. It's her classroom and you are taking her place. In their warped minds you might become a symbol of her. Oh, not you especially. It would be so with anyone who had taken her place."

"Am I supposed to be frightened?"

"You'd be some kind of nut if you weren't—just a little," smiled Buck for the first time in several minutes.

"I'll cross that bridge when I come to it."

"Juvenile delinquents," mumbled Mr. Carter. "She said they were. They all wore masks. The whole kit and kaboodle of them should be locked up."

"It's certainly apparent many of them are not interested in school," Miss O'Hara said softly. "In the two days I've been here I've had to keep on an average of four boys a day in after school."

"Ahh," said Buck strongly. "There we put another point strongly against you. Maybe the boys didn't like being kept after school."

"The little b..." and Mr. Carter caught himself. "They have to be punished. Miss O'Hara was perfectly in the right in doing what she had to do."

"I don't deny that."

"Then what are you driving at Buck?"

"I only say, it's one more point we've got to look out for. It might very well have triggered the actions that happened in this room tonight." Miss O'Hara came forward seriously. "Are you implying that I'm responsible for this?"

Buck calmed her. "Not in the usual sense of the word. You see, any little thing can trigger a warped mind. Those who would murder a helpless woman such as Miss Long certainly wouldn't stop at wrecking a school room or burning a car."

"And my keeping certain ones after school could be directed to violence?" June O'Hara was not angry. She was interested. It was an all new adventure to her as in the past five years as a teacher she had always had sedate, well protected schools, with mostly well behaved children. This type of affair was all new to her and she had an open mind for the advice of those in authority who know.

"You're teaching a rowdy class in a rough school in the toughest gulf port town in Texas. Most of these kids don't appreciate going to school during the proper school hours Let alone one minute longer. It all adds up to their retaliation against authority. You've got a bad bunch, Miss O'Hara. A lot of them bad—through and through." Again Buck let his arm sweep slowly around the wrecked room. "The ones who did this have no respect for anyone or anything with a sign of authority."

"You're wrong about that, Sheriff Rhodes," she said simply, then turned and indicated the flag still neatly placed in its standard. "The flag hasn't been touched."

CHAPTER FOUR

Reverend Steele looked ahead to the gaudily-lit street which spread out, ahead of him, toward the black Gulf waters beyond. He shook his head sadly. Not because of the dozen or more beer joints and the same amount of bottle shops, or the red light district, or even the people. "Weak is the flesh," he quoted silently. It was the street itself which vexed him. As dirty a street as had ever lined the march of a trail drive was the only way it could be explained. There was never anyone who wanted to see something done about it. A year before he tried to get the merchants to pool some money and rebuild and remodel, and with a second choice, each one could take care of his own frontage. The plans never got off the ground. None of the merchants felt their profit justified any added expense. With the truth of the matter laid at the fact they were getting all the profit that could be gotten out of the area as it was. Why should they dish out anymore expenditures! And who in hell cared what the street or the front of the buildings looked like—certainly not the customers.

Light moans of pleasure from a man and a woman issued from an alley and he stopped. He tried to penetrate the deep blackness, but it was impossible and there was no point in an investigation. He knew what was going on. A dirty blanket or a discarded mattress, stretched out in the alley filth. A man and a woman, probably drunks or bums, maybe a street walker and her john; possibly a couple of teenagers. Once he had investigated such an affair; he had the jagged knife scar in his side to prove it.

Reverend Steele turned his footsteps back to the street. A crowded street but a lonely one. He accepted a greeting here and there from well-wishers, but those were few and far between. The single theatre was doing a capacity business for its double horror feature bill, and he recognized a few of the teenagers waiting in the lobby for seats. He gave his usual, friendly gesture which, also as usual, was greeted by the turning of their backs to him. He hadn't expected any different. It had become the general thing to do. He was a symbol of all they had come to reject. In most cases they didn't know why the rejection, but it had started somewhere and steadily grew until it was the thing to do.

His footsteps passed a couple of beer joints then he paused in front of the large plate glass window which denoted Jockey's Place. A hamburger and coke joint owned by a short man, almost a midget, who in his earlier years had been a race car driver and jockey of some renown. Then there was his final fall in a stretch run which crippled his left leg and put him out of the sports world for good. Jockey's Place boasted a ten stool counter and several wooden tables and chairs with carved initials and symbols scratched there by the hordes of teenagers who, over the years, frequented there to hear Jockey tell his exciting adventures; most of which were tall tales from his fertile mind, but his face and name on many sports posters plastered on the walls, gave credence to his stories.

The real color in the place came from a multicolored jukebox with blinking lights, which blared the latest teenage conception of music. Although Reverend Steele didn't approve of the Place's atmosphere, he could find no harm in Jockey who seemed to be a right sort, misguided perhaps, but a right sort. It was better that the kids gathered there than on street corners. Jockey served no beer in the Place, and Reverend Steele knew for a fact Jockey had personally, and violently, turned down all offers of gambling devices and other paraphernalia which might tend to demoralization of the juveniles. Jockey wasn't the best influence on the younger set, but then again he was far from being the worst.

Reverend Steele walked on again, another block, until he saw a rather plump woman in her late fifties. Her faded house dress, but clean apron, floated around her knees as she swept the street in front of her small delicatessen.

"Good evening, Mrs. Purdue," the clergyman greeted her pleasantly.

The woman stopped her sweeping action and looked with tired eyes to the smiling man. "What's so good about it Reverend Steele? My back is killing me, my feet are so bad I can hardly stand in shoes. My ulcers will be putting me in the hospital again one of these days. Nothing but work,

work, work, all the time. Twelve hours a day in the store, alone since the mister went to his rewards... can't find Rhoda no place... she don't like the store you know. Her own dear departed father's delicatessen that was responsible for bringin' her up, feedin' and clothin' her, and she can't stand the sight of it. It just ain't good enough for her now. A salami, she says, is for the jerks—oh, that girl of mine..." Then a sudden hope sprung into her eyes. "Have you seen her tonight, Reverend?"

"As a matter of fact I did," he said, then added. "But it was perhaps an hour or more ago."

Mrs. Purdue's face fell again. Her voice was hard in the honesty she felt. "With them tramps she's been hangin' around, I'll bet!"

Caught off guard momentarily, Reverend Steele let his own eyes drop briefly. "Well... she was with girlfriends."

Mrs. Purdue threw up her hands, then let the end of the broom settle back to the sidewalk again. "Just as I thought. Them tramps." The woman shook her finger in Reverend Steele's face. "Mark my words! Rhoda is gonna turn out just like her sister Lila. Just like Lila," she emphasized. "Spendin' the rest of her days in jail."

"Now, now, Mrs. Purdue. Rhoda is not a bad girl. She has never been in any serious trouble. You must realize Mrs. Purdue, she is growing. Things which were pleasant to her once may not mean the same any longer. As they grow they have more interests…"

"Sure… she's got interests… like hangin' around street corners with the tramps…"

"There is good in all of us."

"I ain't talkin' about folks like us. I'm talkin' about them, Reverend Steele." Then again hopeful. "Can't you get my Rhoda goin' to one of your clubs or somethin'?"

"I'd like nothing better than to do just that."

"She won't go!"

"Rhoda has a very strong mind of her own."

Mrs. Purdue shook her broom. "Maybe I should weaken her mind a little with this."

"I don't think that would be the right psychology."

"Ha! Psychology. Meterology—Salami! Twenty years ago we used this," and once more she waved the broom. "You didn't hear about none of the things like goin' on today with the kids."

"Perhaps you have something there Mrs. Purdue." And he meant it. Many had been the time he'd have liked to just grab out and shake the love of God into some brat's head, or taken a paddle to beat the devil out of their pants. "In the meantime, I think we'll have to do it in the present, more conventional way."

"You think the way you like Reverend, and do it. And I'll do the way I think it. And I think everybody today got it all wrong. The kids got it too easy. Too easy to make money, to get cars, to leave home. But someday I take her over my knee and put the paddle where it belongs…

I'd…" But she cut off and let a coy smile come to her plump features. "Reverend Steele. Would you like to see the birthday present I got for my Rhoda?"

"Is it her birthday?"

"Saturday!"

Reverend Steele affixed his most glowing smile. "Mrs. Purdue, I would like nothing better than to see what you're giving her."

Soundlessly she turned and entered the well-lighted delicatessen. She leaned the broom up against the door and led the clergyman through the thin aisle between counter and refrigerated, glass-enclosed meat dispensers. Cheeses and salami along with straw-covered wine bottles hung from the ceiling, making a perfume of its own. At the rear of the establishment she opened a small door to a stairway which led to her living quarters on the second floor. "Forgive the place, Reverend. With all the work in the store I don't have but Sunday afternoon to do my cleaning…" She glanced back to him. "Sunday is my only day."

"I understand, Mrs. Purdue."

"After church, you know…"

"Of course, Mrs. Purdue."

The second floor living quarters were comfortable and clean, aside from Mrs. Purdue's apologies. The furniture undoubtedly had been purchased at the time she and Mr. Purdue had been married, it was old and faded, showing the usage of the years. But she had kept it in good repair. "Some coffee?" she asked as they passed through the kitchen toward a back bedroom.

"No thank you, not just now, Mrs. Purdue."

Her room, her bedroom, held a scarred wooden chair, a four-poster bed and a night stand with a cross. Reverend Steele removed his felt hat in reverence, remembering suddenly he should have taken it off when he first got to the stairway leading to the lady's rooms. However, Mrs. Purdue took it for a religious meaning as she saw his gaze. "Sometimes, He is my only comfort," she said with deep respect and meaning. Then she reached down under her bed and brought out a large department store-type box. Carefully, she untied the ribbons, then took the lid from the box. She held up a fluffy party dress of pale blue. "Maybe, you think, she'll like this? For the dances sometimes she goes to?"

"My, it is lovely. Rhoda should be so pleased."

Mrs. Purdue's wide grin of pleasure turned to a sad smile. "I hope so, Reverend. I so much hope so. She's wanted a new party dress like this for so long. Maybe I should have gotten it for her a long time ago—but it was so expensive, even on sale, and what with the funeral of her dear father, and—and the other expenses. There was many other uses for our little money. I had to save and save and save."

Reverend Steele put his arms around the woman's shoulder comfortingly. "She will appreciate it much more now. After all, had she received it previously, the surprise and the joy of the occa-

42

sion would already be in the past. Gone—never to be realized again. Now, the joy is yet to be looked forward to."

For a moment Mrs. Purdue was puzzled, then she broke out in peels of laughter which made her rolly-polly belly shake in all directions. "Oh, Reverend. Ain't you the one! You can change anybody's feelin's in just one second, the way you talk. You could make the devil forget he's an enemy of the Lord with your words."

Reverend Steele joined her in laughter. "That, my dear Mrs. Purdue, I wish I could make an immediate fact." He turned toward the door. "But now I must be going. I still have much to accomplish tonight."

"Sure. Sure, Reverend. I know how such a busy man you are." She carefully laid the dress on the bed. "Reverend?"

He turned to her. "Yes?"

She spoke slowly. "My Lila wasn't always such a bad girl. Once... once she was a nice girl. She worked hard. She got in with them tramps. She was not always a bad girl."

"Of course, she wasn't, Mrs. Purdue. Even now I hear reports that she is doing fine. Taking her medicine and giving no one any trouble. She's taking up a trade... knitting, I believe." Reverend Steele hadn't heard a word about the girl since her trail and conviction, but what was a little white fib if it would make an old woman have faith.

"She will never come home."

"There is always hope. And when she does,

43

she will be a different girl."

"I would like to believe that."

"Have faith."

"I have faith. But the Judge said what was to be."

"If she is rehabilitated, there is always the possibility of a change."

"Yes… yes…" She walked to the door near him. "I would not want her back here. She would not be good for my Rhoda. But I do not like for her to be behind bars all the rest of her life. She is young…"

"I will do all I can to help."

"Thank you, Reverend." She paused briefly as he started out again. "Should you see my Rhoda, tell her I want her to come home."

"I'll do that, Mrs. Purdue." And he went down the stairs, out through the delicatessen and back to the street.

CHAPTER FIVE

Lila Purdue waited patiently in the prison hospital. She kept telling herself, over and over, "This is the night. This is the night." And how well she had planned it. Then on top of her own plans more luck befell her. She learned most of the hospital staff would be attending a convention, and she would be in the hospital on that night. Entrance to the hospital had been easy. She simply inflicted a deep gash on her left leg with a pair of scissors while at her job on the sewing line: an accident caused by her tripping as she rose from her chair to get a drink of water. It was all proper and above suspicion. The gash had been deep enough to cause hospitalization for a day or two, but not so deep as to cause any permanent damage.

She smiled as she looked around the darkened hospital ward listening to the sounds of sleep, the snoring and the deep breathing. The others had been asleep for hours, but she had no trouble in keeping awake. The thoughts of being on the other side of the fence gave her all the strength she needed to keep her eyes open and her wits about her. Beneath the sheet and light blanket she had been flexing the muscles of her injured leg for hours so they wouldn't tighten or become stiff. A stiff leg was one thing she could do without later. There had been some pain in the beginning, but the doctor gave her a shot which killed that immediately. She had also been given

45

a sedative which she refused. All in all she was feeling quite good. Why shouldn't she? Very soon she would be kissing those high grey walls goodbye. There were no walls at the front entrance of the hospital. Only a locked door to which each of the nurses and the doctors had a pass key, just like the matrons. There were no guards in the hospital, only outside the front door, and even then they wouldn't bother anyone who came out using a key; at least they wouldn't check very closely. But she also knew her movements had to be swift and sure. She wouldn't get a second chance.

The chance came during the ward nurse's ten-thirty rounds. The nurse was the one Lila had hoped for. Her name was Mary and she was about the same size as Lila. She flashed her light into each of the sleeping faces until finally the light fell on Lila's open eyes and bright smile. "Hello," she said.

"Still awake?" whispered the nurse, then looked at Lila's chart on the foot of the bed. "The doctor says here you can have a sleeping pill if you want."

"No thank you. I don't like taking pills." Lila assumed her best behavior and tones. "I only woke up when you came in," she lied.

"Alright. It's always better if you don't have to take sleeping pills."

"Sure, Nurse Mary. But I do gotta take a crap." She took her hands from behind her head and sat up.

Nurse Mary was disgusted at the sound of the

46

word even though it was part of the daily expressions, as much in use as the word coffee. "I'll get you a bedpan. Please don't curse."

"Holy God in Heaven! Did you ever try to take a crap in one of them things?" She felt she had played it pretty smart. "There, is that better." Then she assumed her sweet-as-sugar voice again.

"I can walk to the shed house, with a little of your arm to help me."

Again the nurse looked to the chart.

"You ain't gonna find nothin' on that chart that says I can or can't take a crap."

The nurse sighed and moved to the side of the bed. She tossed the blanket and the sheet back and helped Lila to put her legs over the side. "Now be very careful, we don't want that leg opening up again."

"Neither do I sister," and Lila was smiling inwardly at her own private thoughts.

"Your slippers are just below your feet," indicated the nurse.

"See. They even got slippers for me. That proves they don't care if I walk to the toilet or not. Who in hell can take a crap in a bedpan anyway?"

Nurse Mary finally laughed softly. "I'm afraid I must agree with you Lila. And yes, I have attempted to use a bedpan."

"Pretty crappy, ain't it? You know, somebody come up with a new kinda' model, I bet they could make a million dollars on it."

"Why don't you work on that in your spare time?"

"I don't have any spare time." Her eyes narrowed. "The judge gave me hard labor. You should read the record."

Lila slipped into her slippers and put her arm around the nurse's shoulder. She feigned more of a limp than she actually felt so that the nurse's attention would be completely undivided. "Are we going slow enough?" she asked helpfully.

"Sure! Sure, fine…"

The bathroom door had no more than barely closed behind them when Lila's free hand came up with all her might. It caught Nurse Mary smack in the throat. She gasped suddenly for air, her hands clawing at her throat, and at the same time Lila threw her doubled up right fist into the girl's stomach. Nurse Mary sunk to the floor without another sound. But even though unconscious, her mouth opened and closed rapidly as she fought for air.

Moments later Lila had dressed in the nurse's uniform, cap, slip and shoes. She had used the brassiere to tie the girl's hands behind her back. One end of a nylon stocking tied her feet while the other end was fastened to the water pipes high over their heads. Nurse Mary hung naked, upside down, like a slaughtered pig. The girl's panties were stuffed into her mouth and secured there by the second nylon stocking. All Lila's preparations, however, had been little more than a waste of time. Nurse Mary silently choked to death even before she had been strung upside down.

Lila looked back approvingly to her silent victim, then assumed the poise and walk she had studied of Nurse Mary, which she affected as she walked through the corridors until she found a room marked "NURSES' ROOM". Cautiously she opened the door and looked inside. There was no one present. Her eyes quickly searched the semi-darkness of the room and fell quickly upon a long, blue nurse's cape. Lila quickly threw it about her shoulders, affixed the neck clasp, and after a fast search of the pocket her hand came up with a key ring holding three keys. One was obviously a car ignition key and the other two she judged to be a house key and the hospital pass key.

She didn't wait any longer. She didn't rush off half-cocked, but she wasted no time in making her way along the hall and to the locked front door which was just beyond an unmanned admittance desk. Her first try with one of the keys was all she needed. The door swung open and Lila was on the outside of the high grey walls of the prison.

As Lila had predicted, there was a guard, but again all the luck was on her side. The guard, in need of a cigarette, was some distance away, in a darker part of the forecourt under a tree, sneaking his smoke. She saw his silhouette turn to her and call out, "Nurse Mary?" And from his questioning tone Lila knew he couldn't make out her features, so she lifted her arm and gave a lengthy wave. That seemed to do the trick, because he remained where he was. Later, when it was discovered she had escaped, the guard would have much explaining to do. "Screw the screw," she said under her breath, then made her way through the almost deserted parking lot.

Even at that there were four cars on the hospital parking lot and certainly the guard would be watching her. How much she wished she had a gun at that moment! She couldn't go from car to car trying the ignition key she had. If she selected the wrong car the guard would be onto her as fast as she could blink an eye. Logic had to play a big part in her first decision. Her mind whirled. What kind of a car would a bitch like Nurse Mary drive? She was young. Probably had men around her. She was single. She dyed her hair a deep red. And that was the clue. The red convertible parked nearest to her was the best bet.

The key slipped into the ignition easily and the motor purred softly. It was not a new car, but the motor had been kept in fine repair. So it was that moments later Lila sped along the state highway in the general direction of Almanac, her mind set on vengeance. But the vengeance did not fog her mind into stupidity. She knew she could not retain the nurse's uniform or the car for very long. She would have to get rid of it. Even if another nurse or an orderly didn't enter the toilet area before morning, it was certain one of the inmates would be getting up to relieve themselves. The nurses and the orderlies could be timed, but not so the untimeable movements of bowels or kidneys.

Lila covered fifteen miles in as many minutes. She slowed as she drove through the main street of a small village: little more than a general store, gas station, a greasy spoon cafe and a beer joint. A wide place in the road found all over the country, generally designed as post office stations for ranches spread out in the rural districts. The village was darkened except for the beer joint at the far end.

This was as good as any, she figured, as she drove the car off the road and parked it behind the general store. Deftly she moved to the rickety rear door which was padlocked with a rusted hasp-type lock. She smiled broadly as she gave the lock a swift yank. The old lock came free in her hand.

Moments later she came out of the store dressed in a white blouse, cardigan sweater and skirt. She had taken low-heeled shoes in preference to high-heeled ones for two reasons. First because it had been months since she had worn heels and second, she might have some fast moving to do very soon.

Once more Lila got in behind the wheel and drove back to the main highway and gave it the gun. The village was soon left far behind her, and she knew that soon the car would also have to be left far behind. But for the time being she kept her foot to the floor and the car zoomed over the state highway.

Miles more along the highway a set of motel

advertising signs caught her attention. And when she came in sight of it, she found it to be dark, except for a small lighted sign which spelled out "OFFICE" and "VACANCY". She pulled into the driveway and on past the office to a cabin far in the rear. She waited a long time in the car, looking back to the office, but the slight noise of her approaching car did not phase the manager. She got out of the car and threw the key ring far out into the desert, then made her way around the back of a second row of cabins to the road and started walking in the direction she had been previously driving.

Two miles of walking took a heavy toll on her feet, even with low-heeled shoes. But if she had to, she'd walk fifty blisters on her feet. She was going to reach Almanac and even things out good. Her eyes remained on the road as far ahead as she could see due to an ever present danger of rattlesnakes and sidewinders which left the desert and slithered across the pavements at night. She hadn't gone that far to be stopped by any viper.

Then suddenly the distant sound of an automobile came through on the desert breeze. She stopped and turned to look back along the road, and indeed there was a car coming toward her from the distance. She was reasonably sure it was not a police car, simply because of the noise it made. And she also felt reasonably sure it would stop for her. Who would be so unkind as to leave a lone girl out in the middle of the desert in the black of night? She also knew whoever stopped for anyone at night in the middle of the desert had to be out of their mind. Didn't radio and television announcements always warn against such episodes? Lila hoped whoever was speeding toward her would be just such a sucker.

The man WAS just such a sucker. His name was—"Jan Calmper at your service little lady," he said, then added, "Hop in!" The man who stopped in the blue convertible was slight of build and had more hair under his nose as a moustache and on his chin as a goatee than he had on his head. He was perhaps thirty and wore a flashy sports jacket over a dark shirt which was open at the collar.

"Thanks," Lila said and got into the car before he could think about changing his mind. She settled herself back in the seat and the man put the car into motion.

He was silent only a moment. "Who'd leave a pretty little thing like you way out here in the middle of the desert with the jack-rabbits and the rattlesnakes?" He laughed. "Sure couldn't of been no gentleman."

"He left me back up there at the motel." she lied. "I didn't go for his kinda' jazz."

"One of them, huh?" His eyes dropped to the road.

Lila had been around a long time. She knew from the minute she got into the car this guy had planned a pitch as soon as he saw her. But if she let him think she couldn't be made, all of a sudden he wouldn't be going in her direction. "Some like it one way. Some like it another. I didn't like it another…"

The man's face brightened. "A weirdo, huh?"

She nodded her head, but was quick to add for his benefit. "Now I ain't no blue nose, mind you. I been up the road before. But no son of a bitch is gonna make me do things like that to him."

Jan Calmper got a sudden twinge between his legs. He suddenly felt he wanted to know. "Like—like what did he want?"

"I don't want to talk about it."

He wet his lips with his tongue. "Did—did he put his hands on you?"

"Don't they all?"

"And—took down your panties?"

"Yeah—sure—he jazzed me if you must know. But that ain't what made me take off…"

Jan Clamper was almost panting. "Oh?"

"It's the way he wanted to get cleaned up…" Lila then felt she had gone far enough with her story. "You going far?"

The sex urge in the man was not going to subside easily. "Could be."

"North?—South?—East?—West?"

"Yeah," she said simply.

"No place in particular, huh?"

"Where are you heading?"

"South West…"

"That's good enough for me."

"You're a beautiful girl. I wonder just what is good enough for you. I can't see where any-body would be stupid enough to give you a bad

54

time."

"You tell me…"

"Why?"

"Maybe I'm interested."

He put his right arm out and around her shoulders. He lightly pulled at her, but Lila was ready for the move and slid in close to him. His right hand draped over her shoulder and dropped down to cup her right breast. "Not in the car two minutes and already the guy makes with the passes," she said lightly, and he laughed. But inside Lila was thinking what a silly amateur she had.

"I don't see you pushing my hand away," he said as if he had accomplished the impossible. His charm was irresistible, so he thought. He pulled the car off to the side of the road and stopped. Lila felt she must not give in to easily. She slid away from him. "Playing hard to get?"

"Plenty. To strangers."

"We wouldn't be strangers if we became better acquainted."

"You shoulda' quit when you was ahead."

"When was that?"

"When you had my tit in your hand."

He was taken back sharply.

"If you'd of rubbed it a while," Lila continued, "then maybe you might have worked me up."

"You like your titties rubbed, huh?"

"Show me a girl that don't and I'll show you a girl with a set of rubber falsies."

He laughed, then catching the girl off guard he

folded her quickly into his arms and kissed her hard on the mouth, trying to force his tongue in between hard-pressed lips. When they parted, Lila did not pull away, but she spit her words hard into his face. "You work like a hick."

"I'm from the big city," he protected himself.

"All hicks ain't from the country."

"I'm no bumpkin."

"Sez you!"

"You're the one who looks like a hick," he said with gestures. "Look at your clothes. All out of proportion. Look at your face—no make up—no poise..."

"Poise?"

"When you got in the car—as sloppy a move as I've ever seen. And I'm one who knows."

Lila threw up her hands. "To think of that. I meet a movie producer way out here."

"Well. Not a movie producer. But I do have a modelling school in Dallas."

"Maybe you wanna make a model outta' me."

"That's not a bad idea."

"First time I heard that line I'd just finished kickin' the slats outta' my cradle. Look, buster. You don't wanna make a model out of me. All you wanna do is MAKE ME." She slipped off her cardigan sweater and laid it over the back of the seat. "You got any whiskey in the car?"

"Sure," he said hopefully, and reached under the seat to produce a fifth of good whiskey which hadn't been opened. His eyes never left the actions of the girl. He knew he was going to have some of that. He only wished it wasn't so damned far back to the motel, but then that might not have been any good either because she had left a boyfriend back there. He'd have to take her in the back seat. Well, it would be an experience. He hadn't had a screw in the back seat of a car since his school days. Anyway, this was a pretty broad, and from what he had felt in his hand she had a pair of titties to stand up with the best he had ever come across. He handed her the bottle after he had broken open the metal cap. Lila took it and drank deeply of the fiery liquid. She sputtered, then drank again.

"Want some?" she finally said as she turned to him.

"Later... after."

"Okay," she said and turned her back to him. "Unbutton me," she directed, as the buttons on her blouse were at the back.

With nervous fingers, but trying to hurry, he started into action. It took him but a moment. "There!" he said as if some great exertion had taken over his body.

Lila turned with a slight wink and set the bottle down beside her for the moment. She held her arms out in front of her. "Take it off for me, honey," she smiled, letting her tongue draw a wet line sexily over her lips.

The man could hardly contain himself. He took the sleeves of each arm in a hand and pulled the blouse toward him and off of the girl. She wore no brassiere or slip. The slip had been left with the uniform and the cape in the thought that she didn't want anything of the nurse's to be found on her should she be caught. Why, she actually didn't know, because surely when the nurse was found she would tell who had attacked her. But she had left the slip with the other things.

Lila's naked breasts stood out in all their youthful firmness. The nipples were hard and pointed. At another time she would quite well have taken the man on and probably enjoyed it. But time was running out for her on that road, and she had to get off it and disappear into the outer limits of the world as soon as possible. She stretched the breasts as far out as they would go, as close to the man as possible without moving her ass. "You want 'em, honey?"

"Wow, do I!"

"Then take 'em with your lips... first..."

"I bet they're white."

"What?"

"Your panties?"

"I don't have any on..." She brushed one of her breasts against his hand. "Take 'em."

"Pull your skirt off."

"Get me worked up first... play with them..."

He moved in and cupped the girl's breasts with his hands. "Not that way..." she said. "With your lips..." She picked up the bottle of whiskey and took another slug.

The man gave a groan and bent down to take the nipple of Lila's left breast in his mouth. His tongue ran over the nipple. The sensations went through her body. She fought to hold her self-control. It had been so long since a man had done that to her. The girls in the prison were all that she had had for so long. But there was nothing like the touch of a man, and what he could do to a girl. His tongue raced over to the right nipple and the searing heat raced through her body. She began to squirm on the seat. She moaned, and she wiggled, and she moaned... his hand found the opening between her legs, and with a scream of delight Lila could hold it no longer... she exploded, and she exploded again and her little ass was flying up and down on the seat... and when the last of the heat subsided and he was still working at her titties, she slammed the bottle hard across his left ear. He sunk to the floor with only a slight moan.

CHAPTER SIX

Jockey's voice held the tenseness of his own excitement as he related his story to the cafe full of kids. He told his stories well and his audience was captured from the beginning. With rough, tough kids like the ones who continually surrounded themselves about him, the stories had to be good. They had to be as rough and as tough as the kids themselves. Jockey certainly wasn't getting rich with his joint. He could have raised the prices like so many other places did, but what the hell. He liked kids and they liked him, and he swore to keep his prices to a minimum, well within their reach. He'd been plagued by beer and wine companies, in the beginning, to stock their wares. But beer and kids didn't mix. He preferred the kids. A gang of dope pushers had tried to force their way in when they realized the capacity of his teenage business. It had been a touch and go business for a while; whether he'd be found cut up in some alley or with their dope oozing out of his joint. He held to his convictions and neither had come about.

"And that's the way it was! Fast! Exciting!"

His eyes surveyed the tight sweaters, the leather jackets. Levi's purchased, it seemed, with someone else in mind. Girls with too much lipstick and eye shadow. Boys searching for manhood through almost non-existent whiskers. "That car took off down the track like a bat out of Hades. The tire blew on the west turn. I held her steady.

I thought of the infield and getting the bucket of bolts stopped, but there was no stopping that way. The gas pedal was stuck. The carb link held it because of a rusted release spring that broke. Brother, that was it. I was headin' for the wall on the next turn. Too many people on the infield to risk headin' in that way for a crash stop. I had to hit that wall. Hit it? Man—I went right through that wall!"

"Were you hurt, Jockey?" came a girlish voice from the crowd.

"Hurt hell," came a boy's voice accompanied by a strong laugh. "He was killed, can't you see?"

"Wiseguy, huh?" snickered Jockey. "Well, I spent two months in the hospital and another two with my legs and arms in casts." He sighed as if remembering the incident. "That was a rough time. Hate to be laid up where ya can't move around none. I'm a guy that craves action. Can't stand layin' around like that. Felt kinda' trapped like. Always felt that way any time I got banged up and had to sit it out."

The man who came out through the kitchen door was a giant of a man, weighing well over three hundred and fifty pounds. He wore a tall chef's hat over a completely bald head and a long, stained apron over his creaseless trousers and spotted T-shirt. "Jockey!" he grumbled in a deep, scratchy voice which would have foretold his gigantic size even in pitch dark.

Jockey turned toward the big man. "What do you want now, Chief?"

"Ain't no buns for burgers!"

"You look in the bun container, under the bread rack?"

"Oh," he said with a stupid look to his placid face, then turned back into the kitchen.

Rhoda, who had been sitting nearest to Jockey, took her eyes from the closed door and looked to Jockey. "Now that's what I call a big one, Jockey."

"Yeah—I got him this morning."

"Where do you get 'em like that these days?" asked Babs as she leaned in around Rhoda.

"Came in off the street. Wanted to know if I could use a dishwasher in exchange for a meal. So I takes one look at the size of the guy and realize it would take a month of dishes to pay for one of his meals. Anyway. I needed a cook and he said he could cook. So I put him to work. Said he's some kind of an Indian Chief, so now he's CHIEF cook and bottle washer."

The kids roared with laughter, then Rhoda said "Well, he's sure enough a big one."

"Standing next to me," said Jockey, "he looks like the whole Rocky Mountain."

"So why do you call him Chief?" asked Babs.

"Like I said. He's an Indian."

Rhoda turned to point her remark to the others. "Yeah—ain't ya heard. He's an Indian without a reservation."

And the crowd broke up. Their laughter rocked the room. Then Jockey's eyes looked up sharply as he heard the front door to the cafe open.

Dee stood dazed, unmoving, in the doorway. Her glassy eyes stared into the cafe as if they saw nothing at all. Her sweater was torn at the neckline. The zipper in the back of her Levi's was torn beyond repair. No bruises were apparent on Dee's face but there were many hidden under her dishevelled attire. Although her body had taken much abuse she felt no pain. The drugs shot into her arm saw to that.

Jockey turned quickly to Rhoda and lightly tapped her on the shoulder. "She's flyin' right over the moon."

"Maybe higher," breathed Babs.

"Wonder who turned her on?" Rhoda spoke as she and Babs again turned to stare at the girl in the doorway.

"Get her outta' here," demanded Jockey in a hard whisper. "Somebody catches her here like that we're all in trouble. I never allow that kinda' stuff, you kids know that."

"We'll take care of her Jockey. Don't get in no sweat," protested Babs.

"Just get her outta' here and get goin' quickly."

Rhoda and Babs quickly got up from their tables and moved past the knowing, and in many cases, envious, eyes of the assembled teenagers. Rhoda took one of Dee's arms while Babs took the other then turned her hot rod. Rick sized up the situation quickly, and hopped over the side of the car. "Man, she's stretchin' for the great beyond."

Lonnie leaned over the side of his car. "Get

63

her in the car before the fuzz sees her."

The two girls and Rick propelled Dee to the car, then bodily lifted her up and dumped her into the back seat. Then Rhoda opened the front door, pulled back the seat and she and Babs got in. They pulled Dee to a sitting position while Rhoda put her arm around her shoulders to keep her from falling forward again. The car, in an explosion of twin pipes, streaked off along the street almost before Rick had closed the door. But he was ready for such quick starts, he rolled with the punch, then settled back. "Who turned her on?" he asked as they sped through town.

"We left her a couple of hours ago," said Rhoda.

"Where?" asked Lonnie.

"Down near whore town," replied Rhoda.

"She was with Lark," added Babs.

"Lark? When'd he get back?"

"Don't know," shrugged Babs. "We went walkin' where Dee said and suddenly he pops out of a doorway. Dee told us to get lost. She stayed with him."

The hot rod reached the open desert, then a few minutes later Lonnie turned off the main highway onto a dirt road which led off into the desert proper. "We'll take her up to the cabin. Let her fly it off there."

"She oughta know better'n to shoot up in town," Rick replied in disgust. He turned to look at the girls in the back seat. "You Chicks better start huntin' up a new leader. The big H is grab-

64

bin' this one into flakeyland but fast."

"And that ain't good for nobody!" Lonnie's eyes were narrowed in his anger, but he kept them steadfast on the rutted road ahead of him.

Rhoda and Babs glanced quickly at each other, both full well knowing the seriousness of what was being said. They looked to Dee who sat between them with a silly smirk on her face.

Dee was lost in a blind world of her own making. She knew she was in a car and there were others with her. There were words, but none of them made any sense. The ringing in her ears made even less sense: a high pitched whine that seemed to draw out her very soul. Nothing was unpleasant about any of it, the sensations. There was only a feeling of well being, but it took centuries for her mind to focus on any one thing. The whorehouse and the whores were a hodgepodge, a kaleidoscope of colors and happenings. She remembered the prick of the needle in her arm and the passing of those horribly constricting pains in the pit of her stomach. And while the smack was taking hold she smoked a weed for a quick lift. The whores hadn't bothered her until the pink clouds covered her mind and nothing else mattered. But then it started, an hour of tortures and degradations. She had suffered them before, everytime she couldn't promote the stuff elsewhere. There was the one who dressed in men's clothing and strapped on a dildo with her as the wife. The others with their stinging belts and straps; high-heeled slippers, cutting deep into her back. Then it became her turn to strap on the dildo and take on the snaggle-toothed bitch called Mazie as if she were the wife while the one with the whip cracked her ass every time it came into the up position.

Dee hated every minute of the abuse yet at no point, no matter what, did she want to stop. The more the abuse, the more she desired it and the more powerful her own climaxes. Even in her heroin enveloped mind she could feel the spasms of the other girls and got as much of a sexual thrill at those times as she did when she popped her own.

Then it was over and she remembered somebody throwing the clothes on her. She didn't want to go. She had tried to rip off her own Levi's and something broke and she was tossed out onto the street. She hadn't been ready to leave. She had wanted more action with the girls. There was no more to be had. The others were through with he... that seemed to be all there was to it.

But she was in a car. The cool night breeze of the desert did little to bring her eyes or her mind into focus. All she knew was there were others in the car with her, but she couldn't make out who. She fought to say "Who in hell are you? Where are you taking me?" But the words came out as a jargon of sound.

"Shut her up," smashed Lonnie, "before I stop these wheels and kick her ass from here all the rest of the way to the cabin."

"What in hell we supposed to do?" shouted

66

Babs. "Jam a Kotex down her throat."

"Kotex... Kotex... Kotex..." rambled Dee, then broke into laughter, followed by tears.

"She's comin' down out of the clouds," informed Rhoda. "She'll crap out pretty quick."

"Can't stand broads who think they're so tough, then can't hold the kicks they bring on themselves." Rick lit a marijuana, pressed the end and cupped his hand around the weed so as to get the most out of the smoke. He took it deep into his lungs. He sighed deeply as the sweet-smelling smoke started to take immediate effect. "Man... that's the real weed. No horseshit mixed up in this batch." He shook his head as if to clear his eyes. "Power... power... power..." he moaned ecstatically, stretching his arms far above his head.

"Put one on me, will you Rick?" Babs leaned forward.

He turned to look at her. "All I wanted to do was get in your panties. Remember last week? I wasn't good enough for you then. You just crossed your legs and said I was a pig. I coulda' taken it from you, broad, but I don't like it that way. Suffer, bitch, suffer."

Babs cooed. She ran her fingers lightly through his hair. "Tonight's different. 'Nother night. 'Nother time and place, and I got on clean panties."

"Maybe I don't want to see your panties tonight."

"So you don't wanna see my panties, but you always like what they hide. Butt me, Rick." She

67

leaned far forward, over the front seat and stuck her hot tongue in his ear. He brushed her away and rubbed frantically at his ear.

"Cut that out, you bitch. You know I can't stand that."

"I know," she beamed.

Rick turned to give her the half finished butt. "Heat up broad, you're about to get laid." He pointed off. "There's the cabin."

Babs didn't look to where he had pointed. She knew where the cabin was and how near they were to it. She cupped her hands much in the fashion Rick had done and she too inhaled deeply of the thick, sweet smoke.

Dee's nose twitched a few times as she smelled the smoke drifting past her. She groaned once and seemed to reach for the drifting smoke. Her hand went through the thick cloud and then she passed out, her head falling into Rhoda's lap.

"Bye bye Dee-Dee," giggled Babs, and she let her free right hand drift up under the front of Rhoda's sweater. "Titties... titties... titties," she cooed.

Rhoda held steadfast a moment, then moaned lightly and leaned across Dee's unconscious form to accept the drug-induced passionate kiss Babs put to her lips.

Lonnie watched them with ever-growing excitement through his rear view mirror. "Heat up, Rhoda," he said. "Maybe we'll get a good show tonight yet."

But Rhoda didn't need any more heating up.

Her legs moved slowly in every direction possible. Her fingernails bit hard into Bab's back.

Lonnie snapped the fingers of his right hand to Rick. "Butt me!"

Rick fumbled in his pocket. He lit the pot in his own mouth and handed it across to Lonnie, then went back into his own dream world. Lonnie inhaled deeply, then again without looking back to the girls and their action directly, he said. "Save some for me, Babs." And he stopped the hot rod in front of the old miner-type of shack he had called a cabin.

"All out, all out," babbled Rick as he jumped over the car door on his side, missed his footing and fell flat on his face. He turned over on his back and looked skyward. Suddenly everything seemed silly to him and he giggled like a fool.

"Let them finish," replied Lonnie as he relaxed back against the seat as he puffed himself into dreamland from the cigarette. Rhoda's Levi's fell over the seat next to him and he smiled excitedly as he listened to her deep moans and words of endearment... of never ending love... of feelings no man could ever give her. "Save some for me, baby... save some for me," he heard himself echoing Rick's words, then he closed his eyes and let his own thoughts take over the scene.

CHAPTER SEVEN

Sheriff Buck Rhodes was tired and at eleven p.m. the night was still young for him. He figured all he needed was some kind of race riot and he'd have a complete night. Fire! Destruction! Murder! His town had always been a rough, tough town, but since the innovation of hidden narcotics, their transportation and pushers, violence had been the order of the day, getting steadily worse. He'd requested more funds for extra deputies but none had been forthcoming.

"Good Christ, how in hell can you expect me to keep law and order in a KILL CRAZY town like this has become with only four men?" he had screamed at the Town Council and the Mayor. His words of attack had about as much effect on them as a fly's attack on an elephant.

"Taxes are too high already." The words were always the same, and he still retained only his four men.

Buck looked out of his window, out over his town. "Taxes," he said angrily to himself. "Damn the taxes. Let 'em take the taxes and wipe their ass." He moved to his desk and took out a fifth of straight whiskey and put the bottle neck to his lips for a long slug.

He was so engrossed when his office door opened to admit Reverend Steele. "Long time no see," smiled the clergyman.

Buck lowered the whiskey bottle, but there was no embarrassment in the move. "Yeah! Like all of two hours," the big man said.

Reverend Steele closed the door and moved across the room to sit in a deep leather chair in front of Buck's desk. He indicated the bottle.

"You suddenly have something against drinking glasses?" he mused.

"Only when I'm in a hurry and cussin' the taxes." Buck put the bottle on his desk and took a cigar from his desk humidor. "Want one?"

"Not just now, thanks."

Buck lit up. He let the grey smoke drift up around his head. Then he sat down in his chair behind the desk.

"What's with the taxes bit, Buck?"

"Same old story. I need more men. Every time we get a night like this one's been I get on the same old kick. Then I remember the Mayor and the Councilmen and the City Fathers, and I get mad. And the madder I get... Hell's fire, I need a drink." He took another long pull at the bottle.

Reverend Steele grinned broadly. "Another time I'd join you."

"And you'd be most welcome. I never was a solitary drinker." He put the bottle down on the desk again. "You hosting the Long girl's funeral tomorrow?"

"I'm officiating." He looked deep into Buck's troubled eyes. "Are you expecting trouble, Buck?"

"Hank! Trouble has already started, you know that."

"But at the grave side?"

"No! I guess not. Even these hop-heads have better sense than to come out in the open. But it's

71

like I told the new school teacher. Just because the Long girl is dead and will be planted, doesn't mean they're through with her." Buck got up and looked out of the window. "We try, and sometimes we learn something, but we can't fully learn how the hopped up mind works. With every individual the thoughts differ." He turned to lean his rump on the window sill. "They have it in for this teacher and anyone or anything connected with her. That's the way I've got it figured. Don't be surprised to see that grave all torn up some night... maybe worse. It's been done before."

"My job is with the living as well as the dead. Anything I can do, you know I'm available."

Buck smiled. "I wish you were on the board of Councilmen." Then pointedly he said, "You know Hank, you should run for office next election. Bet you'd make it. Then maybe I'd have an ally for a change."

"Bring that up around election time and I'll think about it," smiled the Reverend.

"Don't be surprised if I do just that!"

"I mean it, Buck. I've been giving it a lot of thought. Maybe I'd also like to see, first hand, where all the taxes you talk about are going. It certainly isn't into town improvement."

"You damned well said a mouthful that time, Hank." Then his eyes narrowed seriously. "You didn't come all the way over here to talk about taxes or elections. You've got something else on your mind."

"Haven't I always?"

"Let's have it."

Reverend Steele let his eyes narrow in a light smile knowing beforehand just what Buck's reaction would be. "It's about one of the girls from Lincoln Street."

Buck was true to form, he threw up his hands. "Ah, come on Hank, not again."

The clergyman crossed one leg over the other as he leaned back in his chair. "I'll take that cigar now, if you still want to offer me one."

Buck went to his desk and reached into the humidor. He took the cigar and tossed it to Reverend Steele. "You'd better take it while we're still friends."

"You have her over in juvenile hall," he said as he puffed his cigar into life.

Buck threw himself into his heavy leather chair behind the desk. "If she's in juvenile hall, that's where she damn well probably belongs."

"We've been friends a long time, Buck."

"What in hell's that got to do with it?"

"We come from the same part of town as these others."

"Sure we did. And as tough a street as any in the country. But we didn't end up in the pokey."

"Maybe we weren't caught!"

Buck's voice came hard. "Doing what? Lifting a banana from Luigi's fruit stand? Painting dirty words on the bathroom walls? Taking a chocolate bar from Hemp's candy store?" His anger at his own thoughts made his words come in a

73

steady stream. "Sure. We had a gang. But there wasn't any marijuana, or heroin, hashish, bennies or L.S.D. in it. We didn't go around knocking over liquor stores and kill the people who run them. And we didn't hold up drugstores to get high. We didn't carry knives, blackjacks, zip guns or even good pistols." His anger subsided and he leaned back in his chair. Both men were silent for a long moment, then Buck said, "The girl you're referring to—Jenny Rameriz?"

"Yes!"

Buck got up from the chair again and moved to the window. He gazed out of it over the tough town spread out before him. "As little as it is there's a lot of town out there, and a lot of desert beyond that. A lot of things take place in it, day and night." He sneaked a look back to Reverend Steele. "Guess your boss the Good Lord is the only one who can keep track of everything that does happen." Again he turned to look back out of the window. "One thing's for sure. This town, as small as it is, has one of the highest juvenile crime records of any town its size in the country. And when we catch them with the goods, like we just did your Jenny Rameriz, I'm going to do everything I can do to put her away for good. Put her right away where she can't contaminate anyone else."

"What did she do, Buck?"

Buck spun on him. "You mean you're ready to stick your neck out for a little witch and you don't even know what she's done?"

74

"Her father asked me to look in on her. He didn't say what she's done. I don't even think he knew. He said your office only informed him she was jailed."

Buck sighed. "Yeah, I guess that could be." He thought a long moment in silence as he moved to sit behind his desk again. "I mentioned the chocolate bar you and I as kids took from Hemp's candy store." Then his eyes hardened as he continued. "Your little Jenny Rameriz went us one better. When old man Hemp caught her at the cash register, she knifed him to death." He made the motion with his hand. "One quick swipe across his throat."

Reverend Steele leaned back in the leather chair, for a moment he thought he would be sick to his stomach. "She... she killed old man Hemp?"

"Just like I said, Hank." The telephone on his desk rang cutting off any more information he might have given. He picked it up and put it in the using position. "Sheriff Rhodes," he said, then listened silently with a growing troubled expression falling over his features. When his hand hung up the receiver, his face was ashen grey.

Reverend Steele forgot his own stomach. He moved forward in his chair. "What's up, Buck? You look like a ghost, and I don't mean the Holy one."

"My night has just been made complete. Lila Purdue killed one of the nurses in the prison hospital and escaped."

Reverend Steele stood up quickly and leaned

his hands on Buck's desk. "Good Lord! The girl has really gone mad. Is she heading this way, Buck?"

"No one seems to know yet how long ago she escaped or which way she went. She'd be stupid to come this way."

"Murder is stupid."

"I buy that. But she swore vengence against her mother."

"Do you want me to inform her?"

"No. Let's not worry the old lady just yet . It's better if she stays in the dark for the time being. That way she can't do something foolish. I'll put a man on her place. Ha, a man," he sighed. "One man is all I can afford, when I need a dozen..."

CHAPTER EIGHT

At midnight Jockey locked tbe front door to his cafe and while going through that operation he called over his shoulder to the chief as he heard him come out of the kitchen. "Hey, Chief. Look in the back of my refrigerator. I got some cold beer hidden in there."

"Me no likum fire water. No drinkum!"

Jockey, with a scowl on his face, turned to the big man. "Who the hell said you had to? Get me one!"

The big Indian grunted and went back into the kitchen.

Jockey spun around fast to face the front door he had just locked as he heard it open. The man who stood framed in the doorway was a young fellow wearing a plaid sports jacket and a porkypie hat. "Hello, Jockey. Long time no see." He looked around the interior of the cafe. "Place looks the same as last time. Can't be doin' much business, Jock old boy. Now if you'd listen to me you could be riding on easy street."

"If I listen to you I'd be riding in a patrol car heading for state prison." He pointed. "How'd you get in here? I just locked that door."

"Hell, boy... you don't call that thing a lock, do you? I got a skeleton key." Then he hastened to add, "But I coulda' done it with a hairpin..."

"Get out."

"Now don't be so all-fired temperish..."

"We ain't got nothing to talk about."

The man smiled, and for the first time a large slash cut across his right cheek. When he smiled it became a deep crease and quite noticeable even in poor light. "Well now. The Boss thinks different."

"Claude, you're always talking about some guy named BOSS. If you got a BOSS, let's hear his name."

"Boss is good enough!" He pulled out a wooden chair from beneath one of the tables, and he sat on it backwards. "And he don't like the way you act. Now maybe we ain't the biggest operators in the business, but we got connections with them, and our stuff is good stuff. Ya see. We get paid off in stuff, and we do like to have some cash on hand, so we take our share of the stuff and sell it. Now, in order to sell it we gotta have somebody to sell it to. Oh, we got a lot of places workin' for us in this ole town, but we want yours. You got the biggest cache of kids. Now take this for the sense it's meant to be. Most of the slugs that hang around here are on the stuff anyway. So why don't you make it easy on yourself and make some good ole American cash at the same time? Then we're all happy and nobody gets hurt. See, Jock, ole pal? Don't that make real sense?"

"Get outta' here!"

"You don't seem to hear so good. The Boss wants this joint of yours."

"This joint is out of bounds."

"Everybody has his price."

78

"My neck is worth more than any price."

"Well now, I can only say, if your neck means that much to you, you'd better start doing business with us."

"That a threat?"

"You've been threatened before. Take it any way you like. Only take some good advice. Don't play footsies with us anymore. We don't like it. Take our good advice and live longer and happier."

"Your kind of advice I don't need."

"Okay—if that's the way you want it." Claude stood up as if to leave. But at the closed door he took a switchblade knife from his pocket and snapped open the blade. He turned to Jockey again, and started cleaning his fingernails with the tip of the blade. "Look, Jockey. Don't you sometimes long for the day, the old days when you could lose all your troubles and bad feelings just with a little puff of smoke, or the pinprick of a needle?" Jockey noticably shuddered in remembrance. "There. you see! You do remember! Oh, we know all about you, Jockey. How you fell off the horses, wrecked the cars, an' all the time you were blastin' off with the big H and the brown weed and probably all the other stuff. Yeah, I know you claim to have licked it, taken the cure at Lexington. But did you really get cured, Jockey? Did it really take? Nobody ever gets really cured. Now, here I offer you all you can hold. You just skim it off the top—all you want. All your troubles gone with the puff of a smoke or the pinprick of the needle like I said, and all the cash you can spend along with it. Think about it, hasbeen. Just let it roll around in your little mind awhile…"

Jockey jumped between Claude and the door so that Claude had to turn his back toward the kitchen. "Clear out, you bastard!" screamed Jockey at the top of his lungs.

Claude reached in and grabbed Jockey by the front of his shirt. He brought the wicked-looking switchblade knife up so that it was pricking Jockey's throat. Claude did not see the giant of a man as he came out of the kitchen, suddenly alerted by Jockey's screaming demands.

Claude was desperately angry. "You oughta speak softer to your betters, HASBEEN!"

Chief hurled the beer bottle he had brought from the kitchen across the room and it shattered on the wall, just missing Claude's head. Claude snapped around to see the giant of a man slowly approaching him. "Keep him away from me," and there was panic in his voice suddenly. But Chief kept coming. Claude spun toward the door.

He pushed Jockey out of his way and stabbed at the door which had locked again by the automatic spring lock. He snapped around just in time to see the big hands fly through the air and grab him by both shoulders. Chief threw the creep, with all his might, across the room to land on one of the tables which splintered under the sudden weight. But Claude's body did not stop its movement with the crashing of the table. It slid with the broken wood across the remainder of the cafe and hit with a sickening thud against the more stable lunch counter. Blood immediately spurted from Claude's nose as it cracked against the fixed counter stools. Then he lay there moaning.

Chief turned to Jockey who had moved in beside him. "What me do with bum?"

"Toss him out on his ear, what else?"

Chief walked to the cowering Claude who tried desperately to find a hole in the counter to crawl in, all the time whimpering his fears. "Keep him away... Jockey... keep him away... you'll get it for this..." And that was all he could say amid his frightened, indistinguishable murmurings. Chief reached over and picked him up bodily. He carried him half-way across the room then with a mighty heave, he threw the pusher through the plate-glass window. "Jockey say you go—you go! No come back no more!" shouted the chief after him.

Claude landed amid the shattered glass onto the sidewalk at the feet of Reverend Steele who had been passing. He stopped and looked down at the dazed man, then to the window, broken as it was, as Jockey and the chief moved in to look out. Claude stumbled to his feet, cutting himself on the shattered glass before running off down the street.

"Good evening, Jockey," said the Reverend as if he had seen nothing to excite him.

"Evening Reverend. Don't see much of you lately."

"Oh, I've been rather busy. I guess you have also been busy." The Reverend smiled and walked off down the dark street.

Jockey smiled knowingly, then turned to Chief. "So okay. You want a medal. You broke the window, so you stay and fix it. Get some old boards from the back alley and board it up. There's a hammer and nails in the kitchen. That should hold it till morning when I can get a glass man in to fix it up right."

"Ugh," the big man said and walked back across the cafe and out through the kitchen door.

Lonnie drove his hot rod up and pulled to a stop just as Jockey was turning from the broken window. He turned back to see Rhoda, alone, get out from beside Lonnie. Her clothes were a mess, as if she had been sleeping in them, or romping with the pigs. "Romping with the pigs is more like it," he thought to himself. Jockey had always liked Rhoda. He figured she was about the smartest of the bunch. But lately she had been getting just like the rest of them. And as Lonnie drove off and she drew in close to him, Jockey could smell the tell-tale odor on her breath. Right then he was sure all his previous suspicions had been correct. "Heard around your mother has been looking for you all night, Rhoda."

"So let the old bat look," she sneered.

"Now that ain't no way to talk."

"Who the hell are you to talk to me like that?" She spit a big glob of marijuana-infected saliva at him. "You ain't my father."

82

Jockey wanted with all his heart to reach out and take this girl over his knees. To pound some sense into her that she needed. "Go on home and sleep it off."

"I want a cup of coffee."

"I'm closed."

"Then open...for me."

"My license says no customers after eleven-thirty. And I like my license. Go on home, Rhoda."

"Ah, you've done it before, for others."

"Never, Rhoda. Never in my life."

"Just a cup of coffee. I gotta straighten out before I go home."

"Other places are open. Their licenses say they can stay open. Mine don't."

"Jockey, I don't like you."

"And tonight, I like you less. You should have taken a lesson when you saw what your girlfriend Dee looked like when you kids took her off. Someday you're all going to get into trouble. And if you're not damned careful, you'll end up with dope-filled illegitimate babies."

"What in hell you know about babies? I bet you ain't even got a pecker left." She laughed as if she had said the funniest line in all of history. "No pecker at all. Not like the boys I know..."

Jockey turned from her and started away, but stopped, as she seemed to be crying. He turned back to her, then walked in close to the broken window on his side. "Now stop the crying and beat it."

Rhoda reached in coyly to run her hand over

83

his smooth cheek. She was trying her best sex approach. "Come on, Jockey. You know you want to do it with me. You always have. Come on, we can go in the back room. I got a stick left. It's in my brassiere. We can smoke up and you can get laid, and I can get laid, and we can travel the stars for an hour, and you can get a good lay. Bet you ain't had a good lay in years... come on, Jockey, you must have some whiskey back there. I got a stick. We can shack together. Ain't that what you want? I see the way you look at all the sweater fronts on the young girls that come here. You got titties on your mind all the time... you can get a good feel of mine... come on, Jockey... I ain't even got no panties on... I lost them someplace... at the cabin? I suppose... who was at the cabin? I don't know who was at the cabin... somebody was at the cabin... I don't remember... Babs did it to me... I did it to Babs... oh, yeah... Lonnie and Rick. That's who was at the cabin. Fun... fun... fun... oh... lay... lay... lay... it's so good to be young and flying in the pink clouds... Jockey, you should fly in the pink clouds," and her hand brushed his cheek again, but this time Jockey was too disgusted to mind his own anger. He threw her hand aside and it slid across the jagged edge of a broken glass splinter still hanging in the window. The blood spurted from her hand. Momentarily it sobered her from the narcotic heights. She looked at the blood, then turned and ran down the street.

Jockey knew he would worry about that hand

all night, but there was nothing he could do. The kid had brought it on herself. There was just nothing he could do.

Chief moved up beside him with several boards, the hammer and nails and an opened bottle of cold beer. "Your beer," he said.

Jockey took the bottle in his hands. "Thanks, Chief." He lifted the bottle and took the entire contents without taking the bottle from his lips.

Rhoda had come to a fast walk by the time she reached the block in which her mother's delicatessen was in. She held her injured hand tightly at the wrist, but it did little to stop the bleeding. It was not a deep cut, but it was long and jagged. Had she been in her right mind, the bleeding could have been stopped almost immediately. But she seemed to take some kind of fanatic enjoyment of watching the blood race down over her fingers and the front of her Levi's. She held a sort of crazed smile to her features as if she were standing far off and watching this happening to someone else, and she liked to watch it. She liked to watch that someone else being hurt, perhaps bleeding to death.

Reverend Steele stepped out of the delicatessen doorway where his figure had been hidden by the darkness. "Rhoda," he said.

Rhoda stopped abruptly, frozen in her tracks. She tried to focus her eyes. "Whadd'ya want, preacher?"

Then he noticed her hand. "Your hand is cut."

"Now ain't that a revelation."

The clergyman took a clean handkerchief from his breast pocket and started for her hand. She pulled the hand away, and he became angry. "Give me that hand." He grabbed it and held it tightly, then with the free hand he wrapped the bandage around the cut. He only let go of her hand when he was forced to in order to tie the knot.

Rhoda's dazed face broke into a gleam. "You were holding my hand..."

"Did you want to bleed to death?"

"Me? Bleed to death? Don't be a punk. I ain't bleedin' to nothin', death or otherwise... that's somebody else. I was standin' off just watchin' the bitch bleed to death. But you was holdin' my hand. Bet you never did nothin' like that in your church. Holdin' my hand. An' I ain't got my panties on. Rick wanted Bab's panties. I bet he's got 'em by this time."

"Rhoda, have you been drinking?"

"Better'n that... much better'n that. An' I got laid, and I lost my panties... and I don't know how many times... and Jockey cut my hand... I stuck it on the glass. An' Jockey wants to make me, too. An' everybody wants to make me. Maybe we can do it on the pulpit, huh, preacher? Just you an' me in that big church of yours... don't get on your high horse... you like a little, don't you? Why don't you get married? You'd have it all the time. Why get married? Get some free. I know where I can get a stick. We could smoke it up. Come on, Preacher... just you and me in the pulpit... maybe we can do it in a casket. How about that old Long dame's casket? We could go down to the funeral parlor and knock off a piece in her casket... you was at the whorehouses tonight. I saw you. I bet I know what you went there for... let's make out in the casket. Then when you bury her you can always remember you and me done it in the casket..."

Reverend Steele hit the girl with the flat of his hand full across the mouth. Her eyes shot upward into her head momentarily, then she spun around and raced through the door and into the delicatesssen.

CHAPTER NINE

Rhoda slept a troubled sleep with drug-induced variations. The creepy crawly things of the grave-yard were moving over her body. For a time she was naked and the things bit into her flesh. Then there was the coffin and she was in it. She could hardly recognize the figure as herself. The creature had closed, sunken eyes embedded in leathery skin, the color of green bile puke. The hair was long, like her own, but grey and kinky with age. She wore a long, very full-skirted shroud, as pink as the clouds she suddenly drifted into. She was running but everything seemed in slow motion and the shrunken heads fastened to long feathered poles blinked their eyes at her. Fingers without hands beckoned her. Severed arms and legs, drip-ping blood, floated aimlessly around her while weird sounds seemed to center directly on her. Then she was running again in the ever-appearing cemetery and there were countless open graves with bodies in various stages of decomposition moaning in a death chorus for her; skeleton hands and talon-like bones grabbed for her. She wanted to scream out but the desert heat that was at her throat, would not permit it, *no matter how hard she tried. It was always that way.* But an added horror suddenly visited itself upon her. One of the creepy creatures got out of the grave. It was a shapeless thing in a flowing gown, surround-ed by dark marijuana smoke. Rhoda knew it was marijuana smoke because she could smell the sickly sweet odor mixed in with a strong smell of sulphur. The thing came slowly toward her. Rhoda tried to back away but she couldn't move. She looked down and saw her feet had grown ankle-deep into the ground and were cemented there and all the time the creature from the grave came steadily, slowly toward her until it was but inches from her face. The ugly, shapeless mouth opened and whispered her name. The smell of grave mould and of maggots came out of the hideous opening. "Rhoda... Rhoda... Rhoda... Rhoda..." Then taloned hands reached out and began to shake her shoulders violently, and all the time whispering her name.

Rhoda snapped up on the bed. She was drenched in sweat. The hand of the cemetery horror had come with her out of the dream. It was held tightly over her mouth letting her frantic screams come out only as muffled gasps. Then the hand slapped her sharply across the face. "Shut up you goddamned little fool!" It was a hard whisper.

The frightened girl snapped back. She recognized the voice but could hardly believe her ears. "Lila?" she whispered as she came slowly back to reality in the dark room.

"Just be quiet!" The whispered voice snapped.

Since Rhoda's room was in the rear of the building, her window faced out onto an alley which permitted no extra light to enter. But Rhoda's straining eyes made out a dark shadow as it crossed to the window and pulled down the shade. "Torch up your bed lamp," demanded the voice. And Rhoda did so immediately.

Lila walked to a large, flowered cloth-covered easy chair and sank into it. "I'm tired and hungry. I've come a long way."

Full realization climbed into Rhoda's clearing mind. The effects of her narcotic adventure had nearly worn off. Her mind was clear and her eyes focused once again. "Lila, it *is* you," she gulped.

"Talk low or the old bat will hear you."

"She turned your old room into a store room. There's two store rooms between us and her."

"That helps."

"How... how... how did you get out?"

"Let's just say I sneaked out the FRONT door when nobody was looking," she said, then quickly added, "and believe it or not it *was* a FRONT door."

"Leave it to you Lila," Rhoda grinned. "You always were the smart one."

"You can damned well bet your ass I am. Look kid. Beat it downstairs and get me some cigarettes before I have a nicotine fit."

"Sure, Lila!" Rhoda started off.

"You got any liquor in the place?"

"Ma don't allow it, you know that!"

Lila's tone became tense. "I didn't ask what Ma allows. Don't try to hold out on me, kid. Now dig it up!"

"Honest, Lila. I ain't got none here. An' it's too late to get to a bottle store. There's lots of wine in the deli though."

"That'll have to do I suppose. Get a coupla' bottles and make it quick. Don't forget the cigarettes."

"I won't." Rhoda took the door knob in her hand but the door held fast.

"You didn't think I'd leave it unlocked, did you?"

Rhoda looked to the key in the lock and turned it, then went out quickly. She was gone only a few minutes and when she returned she had bologna, cheese, bread, two bottles of wine, cigarettes and matches which she put on the bed. Lila grabbed up the cigarettes and hastily tore open the pack. Rhoda already had a match lit.

"Ahhh, that's better," replied the older girl when the butt was going. She looked to the bed then picked up the slices of bologna which were wrapped in plastic. "Boloney! Just like up at the joint." She turned to Rhoda. "Take the cork outta' one of them wine bottles." Then she built a tall bologna and cheese sandwich and went back to sink again into the easy chair. "I killed a broad last night," she said simply. "A nurse at the prison hospital. I thought I only put her to sleep the hard way. Some reports on the radio said I cooled the bitch."

Rhoda didn't answer. At the moment she couldn't think of anything to say.

"Then I cracked a guy's skull open with his own whiskey bottle and stole his car. Who knows? Maybe he's croaked too."

The younger girl shuddered at the coldness of

her sister's reference to her act.

"Maybe you could claim it was an accident!"

"Don't be a creep. There are no accidents in a prison break."

"I'm afraid for you, Lila."

"Good Christ why? I can only get life again, and I've already been sentenced to that once. What else can they do? Cops and their stupid laws. Reformers and their 'Be kind to our poor demented'. I kill and all the state can do is put me under a roof and feed me for the rest of my life. I tell you, kid, the laws are all on my side when it comes right down to it." She laughed. "I have actually got away with murder. No matter how many times—I can only get life. And I only got one life to live." Her laugh was a bit too loud for Rhoda's comfort.

"We'd better keep our voices down or Ma will wake up and hear us." Rhoda was nervous.

"Damned old bat. Turn me in to the cops. She's got something comin' for that little bit of business." Lila ate angrily.

"Ma felt she was doin' right."

Lila's voice came out a controlled whisper, but in it was all her anger and venom which had been building inside her guts for the past many months. "Right? What's right about turning your own daughter over to the cops so they can put her behind bars and throw away the key? She never was in such a place. How could she know what's right and what ain't right about it?"

Rhoda moved to her sister and put a comforting arm about her shoulders. "You're home now. That's all that matters. Forget it."

Lila brushed the girl's arm away. "Forget it! Sure, I'll forget it. Just as soon as I even up the score." She snapped to her feet and moved to the bed where she made another bologna and cheese sandwich. "Who's been runnin' you chicks since I left?"

"Dee took over!"

"That hop head shitbird couldn't lead anybody out of a one-way hole. Bet you ain't got a buck in your pocket?" Rhoda lowered her head dejectedly and sat on the edge of the bed. She didn't have to answer the question. "Just like I figured." Lila moved back to the easy chair. "How do you get enough cash to keep up your supply of weed?"

Rhoda looked up sharply.

"Don't look so innocent. Nobody knows the smell of POT better'n me. And sister, when I come in here, you was stinkin' from weed."

Rhoda lowered her head again. She spoke slowly. "Dee got all smacked up on H in town so we drove her out to the desert cabin... you know the place."

"We?"

"Lonnie, Rick and Babs."

"Babs Halpin?"

"Yeah!"

"Old Queer Babs!" Lila laughed, then became serious again. "Look, kid. She may do exciting things to you in bed, but be careful. She's a real nut. Sure! I've killed! But I was forced into it by circumstances. Babs will kill just because she enjoys it, and it won't matter who it is that's gettin' killed—friend or enemy. She likes blood and the pain of somebody else. That's the way she pops her jollies best."

"I know," Rhoda said softly, her eyes blinking horror as she remembered that night three nights before. "The gang killed Miss Long coupla' nights ago."

"That figures! What in hell'd they kill the teacher for?"

"She'd been giving some of the gang a bad time, them that still goes to school, so everybody figured she oughta be taught a lesson. All the kids wore masks so she couldn't prove nothin'. But all the time everybody was usin' pot or shootin' up on H, and pretty soon one thing led to another. Lonnie was flyin' on H. I don't know if he meant to do it or not. You know him and that knife. It's like a razor. Everybody was jazzin' like crazy, and Babs with the blood bit. Everybody was laughin' and yellin' and jazzin'. A real orgy. An' all the time the teacher was screamin'. I guess by the time the boys threw her on the hospital lawn she'd lost too much blood. Anyway, she died the next mornin'. Probably a good thing she did. She heard about a shipment of stuff comin' in from Mexico. You know Dee when she flies on H. She says anything that comes to her head."

"She have time to spill anything to the cops?"

"That's what we've been trying to find out. Anyway, all she could tell was that some was comin' in. Nobody knew until tonight who was bringin' it in."

"You found out tonight?"

"Dee spilled it again, up at the cabin. We take it off his boat Friday night."

Lila's eyes lit up. "You mean Lark? Lark's boat? Is he back?"

"That's right."

"Now you're talkin' big time." She walked to the second bottle of wine and uncorked it. She took a long pull at the wine then spoke softly.

"Does he ever mention me? Lark?"

"Until last night I haven't seen him in over a month. But he used to talk about you all the time. He used to say you were the best doll in the bunch—when you were leadin' the Chicks."

"Lark!" She rolled the name over on her tongue as if she were tasting something very pleasant. "Now there's a man. If the OLD gang were still together, and knowing what I know now... nobody could ever bust us again." Then her voice became a demon. "First thing tomorrow find him for me. I want to see him as soon as possible."

"Dee won't like that!"

Lila's face turned red with anger. "What in hell's Dee got to do with what I want?"

"She does all the talkin' to Lark that's to be done. She don't let nobody else get near him when it comes to business."

"I'll change that. You just do like I tell you."

"Sure, Lila. You know I will."

Lila threw a remaining crust of bread into a bucket beside the bed, then she indicated the remnants of food on the bed. "Get rid of that stuff. It's been a long day and I'm tired."

Rhoda tossed the foodstuffs into the bucket then looked to the clock on her night stand. The hands stood at four a.m. "It's late. Ma will be getting up in an hour or so. She always does."

Lila turned to indicate the door. "Lock the door and get me a nightie. We only had potato sacks up there. It'll feel good getting into something soft for a change."

"You always did like nice clothes," said Rhoda as she crossed to the door and locked it. "I got a nice one for Christmas." When she turned back to face Lila, her features were troubled again. "Lila? What happens if the cops come lookin' around here for you? They will, you know."

"The door is locked. It'll give me plenty of time to get out of the window, the same way I got in. I got a rope and a hook I made years ago, for getting in and out of my window when I didn't want Ma to know I was out. It's been in the alley all this time. A rope and a window hook. It's easy to climb once you get the knack. I got it under the pillow." She pointed to the pillow, but Rhoda didn't investigate any further. She went to the dresser and took out a soft blue nylon nightgown which she handed to Lila. Lila stripped immediately and let the soft folds drift down over her body. She sighed in ecstasy at the luxurious feeling. "Now that is nice..." she purred, then got in under the covers. She turned to look up at Rhoda. "You better get out of those clothes too. They stink."

"I know. I had a bad dream."

"Pot always ends up in bad dreams."

"I sweat them up pretty bad."

"And the M smoke didn't help any. You ain't gonna' be able to wash the smell out, and you don't dare take them to the cleaners. Put them in an ash can tomorrow—someplace away from here."

"Sure, Lila. Soon's I go out lookin' for Lark in the morning." She shrugged off her clothes and stuffed them into a large paper bag she took from the closet. Rhoda took a long time in putting the Levi's with the other things. "My only pair of Levi's..."

"So you'll get another. I got some dough outta' that guy I knocked over with the whiskey bottle. Hundred and twenty bucks and some change. Besides, wear a skirt for a while. It's much easier to pull a skirt up then pull a pair of pants down." She raised up on one elbow. "You never did tell me how you got dough for pot?"

"I jazzed Rick and Lonnie..."

"And Babs..."

"Yeah," blushed Rhoda.

"So don't be embarrassed. She's pretty good. I been there before you. Just watch her, that's all."

Rhoda slipped into a second nightie she took from the dresser drawer. It was pink, and it was nylon, but much older than the one she had given Lila. She slid under the covers beside Lila, then reached over and turned off the lamp. The smell of the bologna offended her nose, so she pushed the bucket where she had thrown the things further away from the bed.

"Goodnight," Rhoda whispered lightly, happily. She was honestly glad Lila was back. She thought at first she might lay awake the rest of the night, so that she would be ready if anyone tried to sneak up on them. But then she thought better of it. She was a light sleeper and she would awake, and she was sure Lila, with all her experience, would be just as light a sleeper. She would have to be, after what she had gone through these last months.

Rhoda was just dozing as Lila's soft voice cut through the fog of approaching sleep. "Rhoda?"

"Yes?"

"Something's bothering me. I ain't interested in you gettin' to the joint where I was. And murder will put you there faster than you can blink an eye. Where did they kill the teacher?"

"Some cabin in the desert."

"Did they clean it up real good?"

"Just as soon as they came back to earth; down from flyin' around on H. After the boys dumped her on the hospital lawn."

CHAPTER TEN

The next morning, Thursday, came on as strong as a glassine of heroin. Dark clouds began to form in the sky around six, along with the faint sunrise. Within half an hour the lightning zig-zagged its way earthward accompanied by earth-shaking thunderclaps and rumbles. Then the rain hit in a sudden deluge. Reverend Steele prayed all would be clear by ten so that he could conduct the funeral services with the dignity he felt only sunlight could afford. But his prayers were not to be answered. If anything, the rain came down harder and the lightning show in the sky became more intensified.

Considering Millie Long was Harriett Long's only living relative, Reverend Steele was pleasantly surprised by the turn out for the interment. The school was well represented by Hal Carter, Miss O'Hara and several of the teachers who could be spared from their classrooms for a time. Then there were a few shopkeepers and their wives whom she had done business with and had become friendly. A few of the morbid curiosity seekers whom he generally found at funerals he'd conducted in the past were also present. They would be present no matter who was being laid away. He caught a glimpse of Rhoda Purdue, but she couldn't have stayed long, because the next time he looked up, the girl was gone. Reverend Steele had felt from the beginning Rhoda knew more about the affair than she was letting on. But his thoughts were far from being any kind of proof.

Near the end of the service Buck Rhodes drove his sheriff's car to the edge of the graveyard and stopped. He didn't get out of the car, but he lit up a cigar and listened to Reverend Steele's words and had to smile. All the pretty things he said about the deceased when he hardly knew her except as a passing acquaintance. Buck leaned back on his car seat and watched the undertaker and his assistant close the coffin lid. As many times, over the years, as he had seen that action done, it did little to stop the shudder which suddenly went through his body. To fully cope with the sensation he had to puff quickly on his cigar.

Reverend Steele lowered his head in silent prayer for a long moment, and when he lifted it again, the service was over. The mourners got into automobiles and started off about their daily business. Life was to continue. Red-eyed from many tears, Millie was the last to turn away from the open grave and the closed casket. She stopped near Reverend Steele.

"Thank you, Reverend Steele."

He took her small hand lightly in both of his. "These things are not easy, Miss Long. At times such as this you must be stronger than ever before. It is the only way we can survive. Do you understand?"

She looked up, squarely into his eyes. Her voice was low but held a violence of tone Reverend

Steele did not expect of the woman. "I only understand my sister is dead! Mutilated and murdered! AND I understand I am being victimized! AND I understand even Harriett's memory is being violated! Who is to pay for these crimes? We all know the groups who are responsible. But who is to pay? The VICTIMS? It would seem so! Yes, Reverend Steele. I understand." The tears flooded her eyes again as she turned away.

Reverend Steele watched her as she walked hurriedly to Undertaker William's car. The man held the door open for her until she was inside, then got in himself and closed the door. His assistant, who was already behind the wheel, drove the car off.

The clergyman sighed and walked across to Buck's police car. "Guess you're elected to drive me back up town."

"Reckon as how I figured that might be the case, Hank. Want a cigar?"

"Not just now, Buck."

"She give you a rough time there."

"She's frightened, Buck, and well she has a right to be."

"I deputized Herb Tyler."

"The Fire Chief?"

"Why not. He's on the town's payroll, ain't he? What in hell else has he got to do unless there's a fire, and how many of them do we have around here? I needed him to watch the Long place, my men have other duties to perform if this

101

town's going to live through this thing."

"Herb's a good man."

"You oughta have a cigar. You look all keyed up."

"This kind of a funeral does that to me. You know how it is. Yeah, I'll have one of your stogies."

"In the glove compartment."

Reverend Steele opened the glove compartment and took out a cigar, but his eyes also fell on the pint of whiskey secreted there. Buck looked at him, to the bottle, then back again. "Get's cold at night sometimes," he smiled, as the Reverend lit up.

"I didn't say anything, did I?" grinned the Reverend.

"But you was thinkin'. Besides, in the car nobody can see I ain't got a glass to pour it in."

The sheriff laughed hard at his own joke, then turned serious as he started the motor and then began the short drive back into town. "I got it fixed up for you to see your pride and joy of Lincoln Street."

"Jenny Rameriz?"

"That's who in hell you wanted to see ain't it?"

"When?"

"Now, if you want."

"Let's go." Then a quick thought entered his mind. "Do I get to see her alone or are you going to bloodhound me?"

"Nope! I won't bloodhound you. Besides, she

102

might tell you something she ain't tellin' anybody else." His eyebrow cocked as he looked to the man beside him. "And you ain't no priest, so what she tells you, you can damned well tell me."

Ten minutes later, Reverend Steele stood looking out through the barred window of a room in the courthouse which had been set aside for his meeting with Jenny Rameriz. And a moment or two later, Jenny was led up from the cellar that doubled as a juvenile detention room. The jailer who ushered her into the room left immediately and closed the door behind him. Reverend Steele turned to face her.

Jenny was not a pretty girl. Even with heavy make-up she would look like an ordinary plain jane. Her shape left much to be desired and the formless prison dress added yet one more disadvantage to her appearance. It was quite apparent, because of her plainness she had had to fight twice as hard to be accepted as any other more fortunately endowed girl. Wide-spaced teeth gave her feigned smile even more truth to the lie it related. "Glad to see you, Preacher!"

"Are you, Jenny?"

"Well, sure! From the old street. A friendly face and all. Gets lonesome down in the cellar with only old Rance the jailer to talk to."

"Want to sit down?"

"Why not?" She looked to the square table and two wooden chairs in the center of the room. "Which side do I take?"

"Any one you want."

"Okay. Right here on my side. That's where the prisoners always sit in movies. The one nearest the cellblock door. Now ain't that funny, Preacher? I'm doin' just like in the movies." She pulled out the wooden chair and plonked into it.

Reverend Steele took the chair opposite her and sat down. "Got a cigarette?" she asked, and the Reverend reached into his pocket.

"I thought you might like one." He handed her one cigarette from the pack and lit it for her.

"Now that's what I call, good, good, good! I didn't have no money to get any and old Rance wouldn't spring. Wouldn't take my word that my old man will bring me some bread later." She laughed. "Old Rance still thinks bread is something you eat." She laughed harder. "Man, how can anybody be that dumb?"

"Rance is an old man." Then he added slowly, "But don't try to put one over on him. He's a tough nut to crack when he wants to be."

"Ahh," she shrugged. "I ain't gonna pull nothin' on him. I'm a good little girl and maybe I get less time."

"You did shoot Mr. Hemp?"

"So?"

"We'll get nowhere with you answering my questions with another question."

"Then stop askin' damned fool questions and let's just talk over old times and how you want me to join your sewin' circle, or whatever it is you wanted me to join. Tell you what, Padre.

104

You get me out of here an' I'll join anythin' you want."

"Why, Jenny? Why did you do it?"

She puffed generously on the cigarette then let the smoke drift out of her mouth and back in through her nostrils. "Ahh, I don't know."

"You don't know!" exploded the clergyman, then recaptured his poise. "You kill a man, an old man, and you don't know why? Jenny... perhaps you don't realize the seriousness of your actions."

"I know the old fart is dead and I killed him. What more do I have to know. I ain't the first girl my age that's gone to prison for doin' the same thing, and I won't be the last."

"God be with us, but it's true."

"Your damned tootin' it's true." She came forward in her chair and blew the smoke dangerously close to Reverend Steele's face. "Look, Holy Joe. He caught me at his cash register. What else could I do but shoot him? And with his own gun. Maybe if he didn't have the gun in the cash drawer I mighta' just run. But the gun was there and the next thing I knew I was blowin' his head off."

"You needed money so badly you had to kill for it?" The girl went into a sulky silence and Reverend Steele repeated himself. "You needed money so badly you had to kill for it?"

"Ahh, leave me alone." She leaned across the table again. "The old fart lived long enough anyway."

"How long one lives is up to God alone to decide."

"So God decided! And I was the character who put him on the heavenly train." Suddenly she viciously pushed the left sleeve of her dress high up toward the shoulder. There were dozens of tiny red puncture marks, as if from an extremely sharp needle, clearly visible on her forearm. "See them tracks? It takes a lotta' gold to keep the supply of H up with my demand."

"You're on heroin, Jenny?"

"Them tracks ain't from visitin' the blood bank. An' I ain't tellin' you somethin' the fuzz don't already know. You should of seen them around here early this morning when I needed a shot. I screamed and hollered so loud they thought I was dyin'. They got a real helpful doc around here. He fixed me right up." She pulled her sleeve back into place and settled in the chair again. "Now go on... beat it... leave me alone."

"Jenny, for a long time it's going to be very difficult for YOU to be left ALONE. You have a tough road to travel, and you're going to need a friend or two to walk along it with you... that is if you're going to go the distance."

For the first time since they began their interview Jenny became very quiet, as if for the first time realization of her future was slowly taking effect. Her eyes lowered and her fingers nervously entwined through each other. She spoke through loose lips which twitched slightly but noticeably. Her words came out slowly in almost a mono-

106

tone. "Don't get the idea I'm scared. I ain't never been scared in all my life," she said to the table, then looked up again. She studied the clergyman's face as she spoke again. "Do... do you think they'll put me away for a long time?"

Reverend Steele nodded. "Yes, Jenny! For a very long time."

"All my life I've been a loser! First I was born and my mother died having me. So I lost! Then Pa didn't want nothin' to do with me. He'd work a day and booze it up two. Ain't that a loss? Grandma brought me up with a bamboo cane until she died. The old bitch was mean. Just plain mean. I spit on her grave at the funeral. The priest slapped me so hard I fell into her grave. Now ain't that somethin', preacher? Fallin' in that grave scared hell outta' me for a long time. I ran away. I was only eleven then. So when they caught me and brought me back, I got the cops' summer camp for two months. Camp! Ha! A cat-o-nine-tails for supper every night. I lost again! A pound of ass a night and I don't know how much blood!

"Then Pa moved in with Ma's sister, my aunt. That way he could work one day and likker it up three. They shacked up like they was married, but they never did see no preacher to make it legal. Aunt Flossy didn't like me neither. The bitch! When she wasn't workin' she was in the sack with Pa or whoever happened to be handy. She kicked me out of the house most of them times, but there was a big keyhole. I watched until it bored me." She suddenly became silent as she fought back tears. She nibbled nervously at her lower lip.

Reverend Steele got up and moved to a water cooler. He drew a paper cup full and took it back to the girl. She took it in her hands but only sipped of the water then set it down upon the table. "When the other girls were datin' and havin' fun." She shook her head. "Not me! I was shook off like I had the crud or somethin'. That's when I lost most of the things school mighta' give me. It just ain't no fun bein' alone all the time. Then one day I took a long look in the mirror and I got the shock of my life. I guess I really took a good look at myself for the first time... I saw an ugly creature starin' back at me... seein' me as everybody else was seein' me... an ugly creep. I cried a long time. I walked and I cried. But then I met some kids who didn't care what I looked like, and there were ways of losin' yourself and havin' fun that I never heard of before.

"In the beginnin' I didn't need any money." She looked Reverend Steele straight in the eyes— hard. "That was in the beginnin', with weed and bennies. Then those gimmicks did nothin' for me. That's the trouble once you get started on the fly gimmicks. You always need something stronger. The first few pops on the H I got for a little sack-time with the boys. Maybe I wasn't good in the face, but the boys said I was good in bed." She looked away again. "Then I needed bread and more bread. I was hooked on the stuff and

nobody was givin' me any for sacktime anymore. I had to pay. I didn't have any gold and
there was only one way to get it." She indicated
the room. "Now this. Here I am. For we who are
about to die. I read that someplace, I forget where.
Maybe in school, I don't know."

She stopped abruptly. She drank the remainder of the water then crossed to the water tank.
She crumpled the paper cup and tossed it listless-
ly into the waste basket. "I'm just a born loser!"

Reverend Steele leaned back in his chair. He
felt as if he had been dragged through a ringer.
The girl had bared her soul to him and he felt
much like a priest at the confessional. But he was
no priest. He was not bound by the vows of the
confessional. But he felt bound to inform the girl
of that fact before she continued. He spoke softly.
"I'm not a priest, Jenny. You know, anything you
tell me… I am not bound to secrecy."

She turned slowly from the water cooler to
face him. "That's alright," she said. "Everybody
knows most of it anyway. Besides. When that old
priest slapped me into Grandma's grave I never
went to church again for any reason. I guess I just
ain't got no religion."

"Do you want to tell me who was with you?"

"I think I want to die."

"You mustn't talk that way."

"But I mean it."

"You don't. Not really! You're a bit disturbed,
mixed up now, but you'll be alright again as soon
as you decide to face up to your obligations."

Jenny crossed back to stand beside Reverend Steele's chair. "Reverend Steele, I've killed an old man—a very old man. I'm in a hopeless situation. I'll be tried and convicted and set to a juvenile home until I'm twenty-one, then on to some prison for the rest of my life. I'm not lookin' forward to that. I'd rather be dead!"

"That is no attitude for you to be taking. You've got to pull yourself together. You've got to think differently. You can never be any good even to yourself if you don't."

"It's easy for you to talk. You're not the one who is goin' to prison."

Reverend Steele's eyes narrowed, but softened at the same time in making his point. "Jenny! I am also not the one who murdered." He watched her as the words sunk in, and then she went back around the table and sat down again. "When one breaks the law, one must be punished," he added, just as softly.

Jenny was silent for a long time and the Reverend respected her silence. He let her take her own time. When she finally spoke she sounded very tired. "Can I go now, Reverend? I'm very tired."

"Just one more thing. My previous question which you have evaded. Who were the others with you?"

She looked up quickly, defensively. "I was alone. There wasn't anybody else with me. Nobody but me. I needed bread for junk. Old man Hemp caught me and I shot his head off with his own gun. He fell down and I just stood there like a drownin' junkie. At least a damned stupid junkie anyway. Then the police came and HERE I am."

"The police believe there were others with you."

"Let them believe what they want."

Reverend Steele stood up. "I think you're lying to me, Jenny."

Jenny jumped to her feet, suddenly angered beyond any further reason. "And you can go to hell with what you think." She spun to the door she had entered and went out, quickly slamming the door behind her.

CHAPTER ELEVEN

Dee appeared to be suffering no ill effects from her previous night's experience. Her long hair was pulled back in a tight ponytail and tied in place with yellow ribbon which matched her sweater. She sat on a packing crate just inside the great double doors of a warehouse on the docks. Her clear plastic raincoat lay beside her, and was still dripping from the rain it had come through, which could be seen pouring down just outside. She liked the smell of the Gulf when it rained. There was something fresh about the whole scene. But when the sun was bright and hot, the whole area took on a stink only the docks of the ocean could produce; she loathed the smell and kept away from the place at such times.

Dee drew her knees up on the packing crate in front of her and filled her lungs with the damp, clean air. The sting of it made her spirits lighten. She realized suddenly her thoughts had drifted off to the same old thing. Dee felt so good all over. Perhaps the dope habit was gone, she wasn't an addict after all. And the more the fresh air stimulated her, the more she was sure of it—this time!

Lark came in through the double doors. He looked back to make sure he wasn't seen; then once more turned into the warehouse, took off his rain slicker and shook the rain from it. He tossed the rain gear onto a crate near Dee and she, although retaining her seat, put her feet back to the floor. There was no formal greeting. Just a nod of acceptance between them.

"Girls over at the place told me you got pretty hung up last night." He shook the rain from his wavy hair.

"Booze and H don't mix. I needed the H, but they saw to it I put down the whiskey." Then she hastily added as she jumped off the box to stand next to him, "But I'm in great shape now. Don't even need a pick-me-up!" She affected a dance-like spin. "Lookee here. Just like on television."

Lark caught her shoulders on the second turn. He pulled her in roughly, close to his deadly serious face. He spoke through hard, tight lips. "Tomorrow night is important to me!" He shook her shoulders roughly. "Get that, broad? Important! And no goddamned hop headed bitch is going to smash it up for me."

Dee began to tremble. Although she had not experienced it before herself, she knew the wrath Lark could dish out. His sudden move to the physical and his hard tones frightened her. She was glad none of her gang could see her flinching under the man's violent grip on her shoulders. "I won't mess it up, Lark."

"You damned well bet you won't." He spat the words directly in her face. "And you're laying off the hard stuff until after tomorrow. You get that straight broad. You may think you're running your devil girls, but I'm running the show."

"Sure, sure Lark. I got it straight. I wouldn't do nothin' to cross you. You know I wouldn't.

113

back to the floor. There was no formal greeting. Last night... I just got a little sick... I got..."

Lark cut her off. "Last night is over," he spit. "You start feeling sick again you take some blended pot so you don't get out of line. Nothing else. And that goes for any of your squacks. Any one of them disobeying my order, you answer to me. Get it?"

"They'll do like I say," she shivered.

For a brief moment it appeared as if he might sound off at her again, but instead he roughly pushed her away. She stumbled backward against the packing crate she had been sitting on. Lark moved quickly to the double doors and looked out, while Dee rubbed her right arm which had been scratched on the box. Then she watched curiously as Lark remained in the doorway, seemingly to be waiting for someone or something. Finally he turned and walked back to a spot near the girl. He lit a cigarette. "Your girls are ready?" The words were absent of real meaning.

"Sure, Lark."

He puffed anxiously on his cigarette then looked to his wristwatch and cursed under his breath.

Dee noticed his apparent growing impatience. "If you're expectin' somebody, maybe you want I should leave?"

"Why should I want you to leave? If I wanted you to leave I'd tell you so," he snapped, and again his eyes dropped to his wristwatch even though only seconds had passed. "It's not anyone you haven't known before," he furthered.

The girl rolled her eyes toward the double doors even though no one had, as yet, presented themselves. When she looked toward Lark again, he was crushing out his cigarette on the floor with the toe of his shoe. There was another long moment of silence except for the heavy downpour of rain. Lark once more impatiently paced his way to the door and looked in the direction of town. Having gotten over her fright of the man and being tired of the same spot, Dee slowly crossed to stand near him in the doorway. She leaned her hand out through the opening until it connected with the rain. Her eyes strained as they tried to see; to get some idea whom Lark might be expecting. Her anxiety was to no avail. The streets were clear far beyond the red-light district.

Both were thus engrossed as Lila's voice caused them to turn around quickly. "A good general never leaves his rear flanks unguarded." Lila and Rhoda stood near the packing case which held Dee's raincoat.

Lark's face broke out into a bright smile as he crossed to Lila. "Take off the rain crap and I'll kiss you." His tone had brightened considerably.

"Then what am I waitin' for?" Lila stripped off the nylon raincoat, and they locked into each others' arms for a brief but passionate kiss. When they broke, she said, "Man, I thought I'd never get to do that again."

He laughed, then turned to face Dee who still

stood back by the double doors. She held a sudden angered look to her face. "Come on over and meet a real pro."

Dee didn't like that at all. She stormed across the room. "What in hell's she doin' here?"

Lark didn't bother to answer the girl. He felt it was most unimportant. "When Rhoda left word you wanted to see me, I nearly fell out of a whore's bed. When'd you get out, beautiful?"

"I'm not!"

"The wall bit, huh?"

"What else? When they locked me up last year they put the key in the first man-made satellite and shot it up higher than we ever flew on the big H."

Lark suddenly turned serious again. "By any chance are you still on the stuff?"

"You kiddin'? That's a pretty dry hole up there!"

"Yeah! Yeah! Guess it would be," he said as his attitude changed for the better.

"Oh, not that it can't be had if you get to be one of the King Pins, or got enough cash. What's paid down here is chicken-feed compared to prices up there. But I didn't have any ideas about stayin' in long enough to be a King Pin and I didn't have the cash, so I took the cure cold turkey. That's the way it is."

"You look just great, baby. Just great!"

"I'll look even better when I get outta' this burg."

"Cops hounding your old lady yet?"

116

She shook her head. " I don't think she knows I'm out. Rhoda's been nosing around for me. But nothin's been said. Guess nobody listens to the radio."

"It's early yet. Don't worry, by noon it'll be all over town, you can bet on that. And another thing. The cops ain't dumb. If they even think you've come this way they got your place spotted."

"I got a special way of gettin' in and out. I'm real careful. I been around."

"You can say that again," sneered Dee.

Lila put her hands defiantly on her hips. "Who's this squack, Lark?" Her words were only to put Dee down.

"Don't tell me you've forgotten little Dee?" he said, supressing his amusement at the game he knew Lila had started.

"Well, my oh my," replied the older girl and walked around Dee as if sizing her up from all angles. "So this is what's become of little Dee-Dee who used to run all my errands."

"Don't call me that," snapped Dee, fire burning in her eyes. But the words fell on Lila's deaf ears. "My oh my! All growed up and ready for a fight like a hen chicken. Now ain't that the king's balls for you?"

"Dee's a real big shot now, Lila," said Lark, still supressing his grin, even though he knew what the eventual outcome would be.

"What do you know about that." She glanced to Lark. "A real big shot you say?"

Dee turned sharply to Lark. There was no

pleading in her tone, just a demand. "Tell her who I am, Lark."

"I don't have to tell anybody anything," he replied factually.

Lila grinned. "Ah, let me tell her what she is, Lark?"

Lark bowed low and made a long sweeping motion with his right arm. "Be my guest."

Lila's eyes suddenly turned to pure hatred. Again her hands went to her hips as she glared at the girl. "You're nobody but a goddamned hop headed shitbird. And sister, that's all you are as long as I'm around these here parts." Her eyes narrowed and her voice jammed her further words home to the girl. "I'm the leader of the Chicks. I was their leader long before you got your first brassiere, and I'm back again to continue being their leader. And if you want to know somethin' more, I don't think you got brains enough to lead a bunch of five year olds, let alone my bunch."

Lark finally let his mouth break into a slight grin. "You'd better listen to her, Dee. She's got years of experience ahead of you."

Dee didn't turn to him. She kept her narrow eyes fastened on Lila in front of her. "She ain't nothin'. Maybe less than nothin'." Her venom poured forth with every word. "I beat every bitch in the gang that wanted beatin' to become leader, and you ain't about to take over from me lessen I'm dead. Beat it, jail-screw." The switch-blade knife seemed to jump into her hand as if from nowhere, but in actuality it had been stuck

118

in the top of her Levi's and hidden by the sweater which was pulled down over it. She had drawn it and snapped open the blade all in one swift motion. "Beat it, I said, or I'll cut the nipples right off your tits."

Lark and Rhoda stepped back out of the way as eacn of the girls held their ground.

"Well, well, well. Little Dee-Dee's got a temper and a knife to back it up." Lila's voice softened but her eyes never left the gleaming blade in the hand of the girl who was crouched and looked like she knew exactly how to use it. "Now why don't you put that goddamned thing away before I shave your armpits with it? And when she made her move it was with the suddeness of a striking rattlesnake. Lila's entire movement was not unlike the rattlesnake. Suddenly she had coiled, bending low. Her right foot snapped forward, and both her hands shot to the girl's knife hand and arm. Lila bent in under the girl's arm and brought it violently down against the top of her right shoulder. Dee let out an ear-piercing scream as the pain shot through her breaking arm and the knife flew to the floor just before her body spun over Lila's right hip and crashed next to the blade.

Before Dee could regain her balance, Lila had reached over and with a sweater-covered tit in each hand, she dragged the younger girl to her feet. Lila's open right hand smashed back and forth across her face until the girl's eyes rolled back. Then she let her sag to the floor. Dee was not unconscious, but all the fight had been knocked out of her.

None of the anger left Lila's face as she retrieved the knife from the floor, then knelt down to straddle the downed girl whose eyes went wide in the horror of facing her own knife blade. "I don't like you, missie," sneered Lila and cut the sweater up the front, from waistline to neckline. "You might just as well understand that right now." She put the blade under the front of Dee's white brassiere. "And if you stay round, you keep your mouth shut unless you're spoken to, and you take orders FROM ME, the same as any of the others." The knife ripped through the flimsy brassiere material. Dee screamed and Lila put the knife to the girl's throat. "I don't like screamers. Screamers cause trouble."

Lark stepped in quickly. He snapped the knife out of Lila's hand. "That's enough," he said simply.

Lila looked up to him, then back to the girl whom she gave a parting slap across the mouth before she got up. "I oughta carve my initials, one on each tit, so you know whose property you are!" Lila spoke when she was standing beside Lark, then she spit a large glob of saliva onto the girl's naked stomach.

Lark suddenly lashed out and gave Lila a resounding slap across the side of her head, which sent her reeling back against a wall of packing crates. She bounced back quickly, her sharp fingernails ready to claw out the man's eyes. Lark snapped the knife blade down, ready for her attack. Lila stopped dead in her tracks. She didn't need her belly slit open before she thought twice about continuing the attack.

The anger slowly abated, but the saliva of her heated anger still drooled from the corners of her lips. "What in hell was that for?" she demanded while she rubbed the side of her head.

"For stepping in where you wasn't asked!" Lark said as he watched Dee, using one arm, struggle to her feet.

"I can step out just as quick," slammed Lila, "I need this lashup like a hole in the head."

She grabbed up her raincoat and turned to her sister. "Let's get outta' here, Rhoda."

Lark took her lightly by the arm. "Hold on, baby." He smiled his weird, self-satisfied grin. "That little slap was only to teach you who is the real boss."

Lila looked at him through narrow eyes for a long moment and Lark felt, for the first time, a slight uneasiness under her glare. "I'll let that slap just slip by this time, Lark," she said tightly. "But don't let it happen again—EVER!"

The man shook off his brief feeling of anxiety. His words matched hers in tempo. "Don't make threats you can't back up, baby."

Lila turned to put her raincoat back on the packing crate where it had been. "You might be surprised just how much I can back up—BABY!"

Dee fought desperately to ward off the pain as she cradled her broken right arm in her left hand. She hadn't dared speak, to interrupt, while Lark and Lila were at each other's throat. But as they became silent she felt this was the time to talk up. "She broke my arm!"

Lark spun on her. Lila had matched wits with him but Dee wasn't about to have the chance.

"You had the knife."

"Next time maybe I'll have a gun."

"And I'll lay odds she could take that away from you before you knew you had it in your hand," laughed Lark, his tensions fading away.

"Easier than the knife, Dee-Dee," said Lila, then she caught up with Lark's enjoyment of the situation.

"Okay," said Dee. "I'll pull out. I know when I'm licked."

"Don't be so fast." Lark's laughter was short-lived. "You have a job to do tomorrow night."

"How in hell can I do any job with a busted wing?"

"Doc'll put it in a sling. You can carry an extra load off the boat that way," offered Lila.

The words Lila had spoken slowly sunk into Lark's brain. "How do you know about the boat?"

"The information is safe with me."

"Sure, I know that, Lila. But who told you?"

"My sister!"

He looked to Rhoda. "Rhoda?"

"I only got one sister."

Lark eyed Rhoda, then swung around to Dee again. "I thought you weren't telling anybody the details until tomorrow afternoon? Only that they would be going on a job."

122

"I didn't tell anybody, Lark. I swear I didn't."

"How about when you were on H last night? How about that, bitch? How about when you were on H last night?" He reached over to grab Rhoda's arm and he dragged her in between himself and Dee. "That the way it was, Rhoda? She babbled out of her fog?"

Lark was hurting Rhoda's arm. She shook her head as she formed the word "YES" silently. Lark let her go with a shove and devoted his full attention on Dee again. "You and your goddamned H. Who the hell else knows the plans?"

Dee was silent and he repeated more violently. "Who the hell else knows the plans?" And still Dee remained silent. Actually it wasn't because she wanted to remain silent. But she was frightened into speechlessness at what Lark might do to her. She already had a broken arm and a split lip. She didn't want any more punishment.

Lark turned to Rhoda. "Who was there, Rhoda?"

Rhoda gulped.

"Tell him, Rhoda," ordered Lila. "He's got to know!"

Rhoda gulped again. "Just Lonnie, Rick and Babs, besides Dee and me."

"I should kill you," he said with deadly softness, and Dee backed toward the door.

"Let her alone, Lark," said Lila softly. "The damage is done and I got use for her." Then she turned her full voice to Dee. "But so help me if you screw up once more I'll cut you up into little pieces and feed you to Babs."

Dee shuddered.

Lila turned to Rhoda. "You get to those boy wonders and tell them to keep quiet or it's their asses." Then she looked back to Lark. "Both those jerks are on the hard stuff too, so they won't talk. And if we need more leverage against them, they did that school teacher in. A word in the wrong place and they've had it." She swung around to Rhoda again. "Make sure they know that little piece of advice."

"Sure, Lila."

"And stay in a spot where you know every move they make between now and after the boat party tomorrow night. Anything out of the way I want to know about it immediately." She looked at Lark. "Where will you be in case of an emergency?"

"On board my boat with the motor running— in case of an emergency!"

"Where is it and how do I get there?"

"I'll give you a map and the radio phone number. I trust you won't be saying anything over the phone we both might be sorry for!"

"Sure. I'll give facts and figures," sneered the older girl.

"What do you want me to do?" questioned Dee reluctantly.

"Go to hell, but in the meantime round up the Chicks and make sure they meet with me at four tomorrow afternoon. Don't tell them about the party or anything else, unless the information has already slipped through. I'll tell them how to dress and anything else I want them to know when the time comes. Now beat it while you got lots of time and you don't have to come cryin' back to me with excuses."

Dee was glad to be on her way. She picked up her plastic raincoat and slipped quickly into it. As she tied the belt she looked to Lark.

"Could I have my knife back?"

"He'll give it to you where it'll do the most good if you don't get out of here and do as you're told!" shouted Lila, and the girl pulled up her raincoat hood and disappeared off into the rain without another word.

Rhoda adjusted the hood of her raincoat. "I'll start checkin' around about the boys."

"Okay, kid. I'll either be at home or on Lark's boat. Now just remember. The slightest thing out of the ordinary about those two creeps you get to me as quick as you can. Check the house first. I don't want Lark's radio phone suddenly getting too busy."

"Smart girl," he beamed.

"Give her the number!"

Lark took out a small card from his pocket and wrote on it with a silver pen. He handed the card to the younger girl. "Memorize the number."

"Smart boy," mimicked Lila.

Rhoda looked to the card for half a minute then handed it back to Lark. "Okay, I got it." Then she turned and followed the trail of Dee as she went out into the rain.

Lark looked to the card in his hand, then gave it over to Lila. "Maybe you'd like to ride out to the boat with me for a while? It's better than a map. My power launch is under the pier."

"Why not?" She liked his invitation and knew what it meant.

He put his hands lightly on her shoulders. "You know, baby, right after the shindig tomorrow night I set sail for Mexico again. Another pick up for the big boys up North. How'd you like to go with me?"

"That's a question you don't have to ask twice."

"Sure. You can stay there, safe and sound. And I can see you when I come down on every trip. Like that?"

She took his hand and led him toward their raincoats. "Let's get out to your boat. There's something else I'd like." She started to slip into her raincoat. "You got some whiskey out there?"

"Plenty." He buckled the front of his raincoat. "And a soft bed…" he smiled broadly. "Just like old times. Only this time not in bedbug-ridden rooms. We have a trawler." He took her hand and they left the dock.

CHAPTER TWELVE

Lonnie handled his souped-up rod with the skill of a race car driver and he might well be classed as such. The needle of his speedometer reached a hundred and ten on the straight desert road and danced between eighty and ninety on the curved mountain roads. He held a sardonic grin on his features during the entire trip and Miss O'Hara, who rode in the seat beside him, kept her eyes on the road ahead.

The teacher was on nerves to a point nearing sheer exhaustion, but she wasn't about to make that fact known. She rode silently, her arms folded over her breasts. She might have spoken several times during the course of the ride, but she had been sure the fright she felt would show in her speech. So she kept quiet and waited for Lonnie to make the first breakthrough. But Lonnie also remained silent throughout the speed-maddened trip. He had looked at her many times to see how she was taking the pressure, but he received little confirmation from her stony glare. There was only the perilous road and the rumble of the twin pipes to keep them company.

Then suddenly, at a great rise in the road, Lonnie jammed on his brakes and in a squeal of brakes and the smell of burning rubber, the jalopy jerked to a stop.

"There it is," he informed as he turned off the motor and Miss O'Hara looked ahead through the windshield.

They were halted on the crest of the mountain road which looked down at a sixty degree angle to the valley floor five miles below. And far below, on the valley floor, tiny lights on each side of apparently the road, flooded the area in a straight line which resembled an air strip.

As if realizing her thoughts, Lonnie said, "It's five miles straight road to those lights down there. He took a short length of rope from under the seat and proceeded to tie one end to the steering wheel and the other tightly to the car's wide wing. "Those lights down there come from my gang's cars."

Miss O'Hara's eyes were fastened on his rope tying action. "What are you doing?" Some of her nervousness did come through.

"Interested now, huh?" he grinned.

"If you're wondering whether or not I'm frightened, you'll never know."

"Ah, you're some kind of a nut fink," he exploded as he tied the rope into several secure knots. "You ain't so brave."

"No one said anything about my being brave. However, face facts. It may appear like you're out to kill yourself, but I don't think you'd deliberately commit suicide." She breathed easier as she realized the importance of her own words.

"I believe I'm relatively safe as long as you're in the car with me."

The smile disappeared from his face. "Yeah! As long as I'm in the car with you." He was angered at her apparent disregard to his mental tortures. He pulled the marijuana butt from his pocket and lit up. The blast of sickly sweet smoke he exhaled crossed under Miss O'Hara's nose just as she took a deep breath. She choked violently for a brief moment, and Lonnie laughed loudly. "They all do that the first time they get pot in their lungs."

She looked directly at him, anger burning in her eyes finally. "Are you smoking marijuana?"

"Well, now, teach. It ain't corn silk!"

"And you're going to drive?"

"The stuff steadies my nerves," he taunted. Then he looked directly to her. "You gonna be a good girl and stay put, or do I have tie you in?"

"You're leaving?" The fright once more climbed out of her stomach and upwards toward her neck, but still she fought it back.

"Not very far. Just under the car. Some adjustments to make before we start off." He looked at her steady eyes. "Naw. You come this far, I guess you won't be goin' no place."

He got out of the car and Miss O'Hara heard him puttering with something under the car, then almost before she knew it, he was back again. "Now that didn't take long, did it?" He smiled. "Ohh! I just cut the brake cable."

"I'm ready, but don't you think you'd enjoy seeing me squirm more, if I knew what the eventual end to this ride might be?"

"That's right, teach. You don't know the scoop yet. Well, let's take it from the top. This here hill is five miles long. A straight road all the way down to that last set of lights down there." He pointed

129

out through the windshield to the last set of headlights far below. "Then, right there, the road takes a sharp left turn. Only we don't turn. We go straight across another quarter of a mile, right across the open field. And what looms up ahead of us there? A stone wall, teacher. A good old stone wall. And this old car goes smack into it. Only nobody's killed... IF YOU JUMP IN TIME. The CHICKEN jumps first. Nobody's ever outwaited me, teacher, nobody. And I got the wheel tied so nobody can turn off the straight and narrow if they wanted too. You get the pitch, teacher. Now we're gonna see who's CHICK-EN."

"We can be killed, jumping out of a speeding automobile."

"You can. I can't. I know how to roll..." He laughed his weird, self-satisfied laugh again. "Your big problem now, teach, is it's too late for you to back out. Just think. You could have been taken care of back at the cabin. Now, your best bet is to faint before the big jump and it will all be over... or hit the wall and be all over it. Yes sir," he finally said. "That old wall makes quite a mess out of a car... 'specially when the car hits it straight on doin' around eighty. But remember, you don't gotta prove you got guts by spillin' them all over the wall. You can jump anytime you want. Maybe you won't get too banged up. Jump anytime you got a mind to... only, first one who jumps is CHICKEN to the crowd for evermore. That won't be me."

"What happens if I win?"

"It won't happen. But if you do? Well, when me and the gang take care of you later, you can die knowing you rode it out. I might even be able to keep the bunch from givin' you a gang bang on the mattress before we crap you out." He shoved the gears home and the twin pipes exploded and the car shot forward, down the hill.

Lonnie had bragged over and over that his jalopy could reach sixty m.p.h. in less than ten seconds. His brags had not been unfounded. The jalopy streaked into ever-increasing speeds. Only the road in front seemed to be visually clear; the road on either side became a quickening blur of undetermined origin and disposition.

Miss O'Hara let her right hand tightly grip the bottom of the seat. It reminded her of a time she had once rode a non scheduled airliner. A two-motored air vehicle in the days of jets. A white knuckle airliner, it had been referred to. She had held tightly to her seat arms the entire, tortuous trip, the same as she then strained her fingers into the automobile's seat frame.

Every crack, every indentation in the ancient highway hit the speeding wheels with the force impact of a pending major disaster. The singing tires, the thundering pipes and engine, the whistling air as it raced by, fused into a terror of sound—a terror the teacher had never dreamed of. A terror she could not admit except to herself. But all of it couldn't be completely hidden from view. Beads of perspiration began to dot her forehead. The hand which was locked so tightly to the seat had become wet and clammy. She wanted desperately to wipe it dry but she couldn't seem to unlock it from the framework. Fright held it motionless. She looked from her straining white knuckles across to Lonnie. The excitement was splashed generously over his face. There was no mercy for life or machine as he held the accelerator to the floor boards. His eyes, a glare of madness in them, held steady on the road. He clenched the marijuana butt between his teeth but the excitement of the ride didn't permit time for him to inhale. The grey smoke drifted aimlessly up around his head and toward the open window where it was quickly dispersed into the rushing air. He laughed drily without opening his mouth as a jack-rabbit stood in the road ahead, transfixed, hypnotized by the headlights. One second it had been a living, breathing animal. The next, it was a bloody pulp on the road behind them.

Again, stomach pressure threatened to explode the teacher's already empty stomach. She forced her eyes to focus on the headlights of the cars in the valley and marvelled at how surprisingly close they had become and steadily grew closer, each vehicle taking its own individual form. Her stomach suddenly belched as she realized the ride's violent end was so near. It was more than possible the last few seconds of her life were speeding toward her shaking body. Her stomach pumped violently up against her lower ribcage.

Her breathing came in short gasps. She bit her trembling lower lip to keep from screaming. She had to speak and the words came in a rush of air. "Don't you realize you're looking into eternity?"

"Sure. Everytime I do it," he grinned. Then his eyes darted to her. "Who's the world watching now, Miss O'Hara?"

The first set of hot rods were suddenly in front of them and just as suddenly they were behind. Miss O'Hara's eyes jumped up to the rear view mirror and she could see each set of cars join in behind as they were passed. They became a speeding funeral procession following the leading hearse. And then ahead was the sharp left hand turn in the old road. It was the turn they did not attempt to make. The hot rod left the cement and shot across the field, slowed minutely, almost imperceptibly, by ruts and holes, the headlights glaring against a stone wall some two hundred yards ahead of them.

Lonnie suddenly threw open his door. "Jump you fool!" he screamed, but waiting, himself, for her to go first.

Miss O'Hara did not budge. It was doubtful she could if she had wanted to. The terror of the wall was only preceeded in her mind by the terror of actually making such a jump.

Brakes of the cars behind could be heard squealing. Lonnie hung half out of the door, one hand on the window and the other on the steering wheel. His eyes snapped from the wall to the girl and back, then to the girl again. In those last fifty or so yards he knew she was not going to jump. "You're crazy!" he screamed and flung himself out of the speeding vehicle, but in so doing his hip connected with the door in such force the rope securing the steering wheel snapped and in the same instant Miss O'Hara came to sudden life. She threw herself across the seat, snapped off the ignition key which killed the motor and with both her hands and all her strength she pulled the steering wheel to the left. The tires below blew in two fast explosions, then the wheels snapped and the axle and hubs ground into the hard dirt. The hot rod slammed sideways into the wall with a resounding kaleidoscope of crashing sounds: tearing metal, exploding tyres, breaking glass. The radiator blew and boiling water shot high into the air. The rear seat tore loose, flew into the air, hit the top of the car and fell, lodging itself between the dashboard and the back of the front seat, directly over Miss O'Hara, but holding the front end of the car from jamming back to crush her.

Miss O'Hara only felt the first impact. The deep black of unconsciousness saved her from further physical and mental tortures.

Lonnie had fallen flat, and rolled over on the ground in time to see, as well as hear, the impact. He waited expectantly for the fire which was bound to explode, but the explosion didn't come. Slowly, painfully he got to his feet. Rick and Danny were the first to join him, with the many other juveniles almost immediately behind them.

"You alright?" asked Rick, without taking his eyes from the crash scene.

Lonnie didn't bother to answer the question. He started hobbling painfully, favoring his right hip, toward the wrecked hot rod. "It didn't burn," he mumbled unbelievingly. "How did those wheels turn?"

"Musta' hit a big chunka' hole... look how them wheels is busted. Your rope tie musta' broke, only thing that coulda' happened." Rick walked in beside Lonnie and took his arm in an attempt to be of aid, but Lonnie brushed the hand away to continue on unaided.

"You musta' run outta' gas," optioned Danny. "That's why it didn't explode and burn."

They looked into the car and none of them noticed the ignition key had been turned to the OFF position. All eyes were fastened on what they could see of Miss O'Hara's body... only one badly bleeding hand and arm, and her left leg, at a grotesque angle under the ruptured seat were visible.

"The teacher looks dead enough," observed Rick.

"Yeah! She's dead! Nobody comes through a smack like that." Lonnie looked at the badly bleeding hand for a long time. When he spoke again, there was a measure of respect in his voice. "One thing she gets credit for. She wasn't no yellow belly." He turned to Rick. "Siphon some gas outta' the cars," he directed quickly as he looked to the many vehicles back along the field. "We'll burn it where it stands."

Rick turned away, then everyone became motionless as the sound of a screaming siren filtered through on the quiet breeze. Rick looked back at Lonnie. "That's probably the highway patrol. The noise of a crackup like that carries a long way on the desert. We ain't got time to torch her up!"

Lonnie looked around to the others who needed no direct orders. They raced headlong for their cars.

"We gotta get outta' here, Lonnie!" shouted Danny. "Them highway guys shoot first and ask questions later. You know that."

The dozen or more hot rods blasted into life and, en masse, took off for the highway. "Get our rod, Danny," commanded Rick. "Lonnie can't run for it with the leg he's got."

Danny, without further delay, raced for his set of wheels and was back to help Rick aid Lonnie into the car, then they took off with all the speed the rod could muster.

An hour later, Danny braked his rod in front of the desert cabin. None of the three had spoken during the entire trip; their minds had been strictly on getting away, keeping their rod at top performance. Then at the cabin Danny reached toward the key in the ignition.

"Leave it!" snapped Lonnie.

"Leave the motor running, man?" Danny was puzzled.

"That's what I meant." Lonnie got out of the

car. "You ain't stayin' tonight."

"I ain't?"

"You gettin' deaf or somethin'? I said you ain't stayin' with us no more tonight."

"I'm beat, Lonnie. I want a fix."

"Then get one someplace else! Come on, Rick."

Rick got out of the car, but he was as puzzled about Lonnie's attitude as Danny was, but he knew better than to ask too many questions.

Danny finally shrugged. "Okay… if that's the way the ball bounces." He shifted into first, but kept his foot on the clutch. "Want me to pick you guys up in the morning?" Then a thought struck him. "Say… what do you play if the fuzz gets wind of this pad and start nosin' around, and you guys ain't got no wheels?"

"One big reason I don't want that rod around," pushed Lonnie. "Ain't no rod around, most likely ain't nobody around. Besides, there's a hundred cabins spotted all over the desert around here. Who's gonna bother searchin' all of 'em, even if they knew where in hell we liked to hole up? That Long bitch was here… any fuzz come buzzin' around?"

"Yeah, and she lived awhile," chirped Rick. "No fuzz knows about this place. An' if they did there's plenty of holes we can duck to back in the old mine. Now beat it like Lonnie says."

"Pick us up in the mornin'," said Lonnie, finally answering Danny's question.

Danny let his foot up on the clutch and his rod disappeared quickly in a cloud of desert dust

137

while Rick and Lonnie entered the cabin. "Shade them windows so's we can have some light," ordered Lonnie and his henchman pulled the heavy drapes across the cabin's two windows, while Lonnie snapped on the yellowed light behind the table they had previously used as a judge's bench. Then he crossed the room to a far corner and stretched out on a canvas army cot. He put his hands under his head as he spoke. "Don't put any snow in mine, Rick. I want peaceful sleep, not the highs."

Rick acknowledged Lonnie's order with only the nod of his head as he started across the cabin to a dark corner, where he pried up a loose floorboard and took out two glassine envelopes of heroin and one of cocaine. Next he took out a spoon and holding it in his right hand he searched under the floor with his right hand for something else. He finally laid down on the floor so that his hand could reach further under the flooring. Lonnie, impatient, turned over to look at him. "You're gonna grab a rattlesnake by the tail one of these nights doin' that."

"I can't find the candle."

"Everything's right in that tin box."

"The candle ain't."

"So maybe it's in the table drawer."

"I always put things back in this tin box when we're through. I always do."

"So how do you know what you really do when you're all smashed up with H? Look in the table drawer like I told you."

138

Rick got up and carried the other things to the table and after putting them down he pulled open the drawer. His eyes showed honest surprise as he took the foot-long candle from the drawer. "Well, that beats me," he said, then lit the candle and let a few drops of the tallow fall to the table so the candle could be affixed there.

"Mix the stuff and quit soundin' off about nothing," mumbled Lonnie and rolled over on his back again.

"We got any water?"

Rick reached under the grimy pillow on his cot and took the glassine envelopes and dumped the half grain of heroin into the spoon, and while the concoction dissolved into a mixture he held it over the candle flame with one hand and reached into his pocket to produce two disposable syringes. A few seconds more and the mixture was ready. He sucked it up into the one syringe, then walked across to Lonnie who had tied an old necktie tightly to his arm, just over the muscle. The veins stood out firm on his forearm. He stabbed the needle into Lonnie's arm several times, and withdrew it. "You got a couple of collapsed veins."

"Keep tryin' until you get a hit. I need the stuff —and now. Right now."

Rick deftly inserted the needle again, and on the third try he knew he had made a hit as the liquid in the syringe started to turn pink with Lonnie's blood. "There's a hit," he said lightly, and sent the fluid into the man's bulging vein.

Moments later Rick returned to the table and went through the same operation again, with the exception that he added a half grain of cocaine to his own mixture.

It was as he had the spoon over the flame that the candle suddenly began to splutter and send off a shower of sparks, much like a powder fuse. His eyes went wide in surprised alarm. Without taking his eyes from the unexpected sparkler, he said, "Lonnie... this candle is..."

And it was as far as Rick got. The candle blew up in his face, in one tremendous explosion which destroyed the cabin with its force. Out on the desert highway Lila turned to Rhoda on the seat beside her. The sound of the explosion was a long way off, but it brought a pleased smile to Lila's face. "I guess they lit the candle. Bet nobody ever flew so high."

CHAPTER THIRTEEN

Lila slept soundly, as if she hadn't a care in the world, but Rhoda laid awake most of the night. Things were moving too fast for her. She had been present when Miss Long was killed, but she hadn't actually participated, she had only been one of the spectators like many of the other gang members. She hadn't bothered going with the gang when they took Miss O'Hara. But she had helped Lila put the wax around the stick of dynamite and adjust the fuse a half inch below the candle wick.

Rhoda let her eyes drift across the bed to Lila's sleeping face and remembered the final portion of the incident.

"How do you know it will be Lonnie and Rick who come back here?" Rhoda had asked. "It might be some of the others."

"The more the merrier," Lila had laughed, that crazed look filling her eyes. "But don't worry. No junkie shares his stuff with nobody. That's Lonnie's tin box where we got the candle. It'll be him or Rick that lights it up. You should feel proud of yourself because you snuck around the other night and saw where they hid their supply. Maybe I can persuade Lark to have a little surprise for you tomorrow."

Rhoda remembered the scene, over and over again. And the more she tried to put the picture out of her mind the stronger it came on, like cinemascope in the movies. She was frightened of

Lila. Before she went to prison she had been tough, one to be reckoned with. But since her escape, she had been impossible. Nothing mattered to her. Somebody else's life meant about as much as a rattlesnake and had to be dealt with. She'd do anything and she did it with a cold, unfeeling heart. No one was at all safe from her wrath. Rhoda wasn't about to try her sister's patience. She wanted no part of Lonnie and Rick's liquidation, but Lila had ordered her along and that's all there was to it. She went along and she helped to murder.

As the dull sun came up and the room became lighter, her last thoughts on the subject were of the stolen car they had used, and the hope their fingerprints had been thoroughly cleaned off. Then her senses picked up the sounds of Mrs. Purdue moving about the hall, followed by the sounds of water running in the sink and the loud flush of their ancient toilet. It had always come through to her as a disgusting sound.

She slowly, careful not to wake Lila up, sat up on the edge of her bed and lit a cigarette. But Lila did wake up. She reached around and took Rhoda's cigarette. "Just like prison," she mumbled, "up at dawn."

"Ma's in the toilet. She woke me up flushing it," Rhoda lied, then lit up another cigarette for herself.

Lila leaned back on the pillow, one arm crooked under her head. She frowned at the taste of her cigarette. "You got any pot around?"

142

"No!" Then she turned to look at her older sister. "I thought you got off the stuff?"

"Ah, pot ain't dope. Nobody gets hooked on the weed. Only when they go to the hard stuff, that's when you're hooked but good."

Rhoda put her cigarette into an ashtray, then slipped out of her nightgown. "Lotta' the kids are mixin' H with snow. That's when they got enough scratch for both. Why's that? Both of them?"

"You sure do got a lot to learn, kid. Heroin makes 'em kinda' dreamy, sleepy. Put the same amount of cocaine with it, mix it together, heat it and shoot up—you go higher than the astronauts, only they ain't got no spaceship holdin' them down," Lila laughed. When she turned serious again, she said, "Look kid, get out and pass the word to your Chicks that I changed my mind about the meeting time. Make it like six-thirty, after dark."

"Why's that?"

"After last night's action, I don't want nobody accidentally wondering where the girls went so early. Besides, the closer to boat time, the less chance of a leak."

"Okay," she said, putting on an old blouse and skirt.

"Then nose around. See what anybody says about last night."

Rhoda crushed out her cigarette. "You'll be here?"

"I won't even get dressed. It's me for this nightie and bed all day. See you when you get back."

There wasn't much trouble in finding the girls to give them the changed information, so with that done she moved about town listening to any conversation she could hear, but it was little more than she was able to read in a newspaper. Miss O'Hara had lived, although she was in the hospital in bad shape, and hadn't regained consciousness. And the second heading told of Rick and Lonnie's accident. The article read as if the boys had been fooling around with dynamite in an abandoned mine cabin. So far everything had worked out in Lark's favor.

Just before sundown Rhoda stopped to watch a hearse and a few cars of the funeral procession pass and she guessed it was old man Hemp going to Boot Hill. Reverend Steele rode in the family car, but he didn't see her.

And back in her room as the sun light faded she undressed to change out of her sweaty clothing and told Lila all she knew. "What do you know about that?" she laughed and the laugh was apparently too loud.

First there was the knocking, then Mrs. Purdue's angered voice came through from the other side of the door. "Rhoda! Who are you with in there?"

Panic captured Rhoda's eyes as she was lighting up a cigarette and she looked from the door to Lila, then back to the door again. Rhoda put her cigarette immediately into an ashtray. Lila quickly got up off the bed. She absently put her cigarette in the ashtray beside Rhoda's. "Well answer her, you dope," she whispered hoarsely.

Rhoda fought to control her voice. "Ain't nobody here, Ma. Go away." She snapped up her slip from a chair and put it on over her head. "Stop bothering me."

"Stop bothering? I'm your mother. I should stop bothering you? I should hear laughs in your room that ain't yours and I ain't supposed to know who? Why the door is locked all the time? You unlock it right now, or I will."

"She musta' rattled that door fifty times today, but she didn't come in," whispered Lila, then ducked behind a dressing screen at the far end of the small room.

Rhoda went to the door and unlocked it. "From your own mother you keep the door locked?" the old woman said immediately on entering, and her troubled eyes searched the room while Rhoda slipped into a brown skirt.

"Ain't nothin' in here for you to see, Ma."

"So there's nothing for me in here to see? So why is it I find a locked door to hide something that ain't here?"

Rhoda spoke angrily. "So maybe I lock it just to keep you out."

Mrs. Purdue raised her voice. "You speak in better tones to your Ma—you hear me?"

"The whole neighborhood is hearing you."

"Your own mother! Your own mother! Listen to the way you speak to your own mother."

Rhoda slipped a white, long-sleeved cashmere sweater over her head. "Ahh, go slice some salami."

"If your father, God rest his dear soul, were alive you'd never dare talk to me like this. It's the punks you run around the streets with that put such filth in your head. You was such a pretty child, such a nice girl once. Now you are getting to be a tramp, like them others. The way we slaved, your Pa and me, to bring you up decent."

"Ahh, cut it out and and beat it, Ma."

But Mrs. Purdue was not about to be silenced. "LILA KILLED YOUR FATHER! She becomes a jailbird for the rest of all her life and you with them tramps are going right along in her footsteps."

Rhoda laughed a strange laugh, one of remembrance, but filled with disgust. "Poor Pa. Twenty-five years ago he started slicin' and wrappin' salami in this hole. He died in the same place doin' the same thing." She moved in close to her mother and looked her straight in the eyes. "And so will you, Ma. Slicin' and wrappin' salami for the creeps in Almanac." She paused and turned to retrieve her cigarette at which time she neared panic again as she saw Lila's burning butt side by side with her own. She blocked the ashtray from view with her body and put one of the cigarettes out, and put the other in her mouth before she turned back to Mrs. Purdue. "I want more out of life than playing nursemaid to a kosher dill pickle."

A sudden sadness came over Mrs. Purdue. "Once Lila said that to me. What has she got now?"

"Maybe more than you think!" Rhoda caught herself. She hadn't meant to say that. But the words seemed to fall on unsuspecting ears. "Ahh, beat it, Ma. I gotta get dressed. I got things to do."

"With the tramps?"

"With my friends."

Mrs. Purdue looked silently at her daughter who put out her cigarette, then turned and left the room. Rhoda closed the door and turned to face Lila as she came out from behind the screen, stripping off her own night dress. "I hate that old witch," she said as if she were talking about slime. "If she knew I was here, she'd scream COP faster'n you could blink an eye."

Rhoda took a clean slip from the dresser drawer and gave it to Lila, who put it on quickly. "Why did you come back to Almanac, Lila?" She paused as the older girl looked to her. "It's bound to be they're lookin' for you here."

"If it's any of your business I had things to finish up here before takin' off for parts unknown." She selected a pale green cardigan and a black skirt which she hastily got into.

"Ma is my business," Rhoda said slowly and softly.

"What's that supposed to mean?"

"You came back to kill Ma!"

Lila stopped the sweater-buttoning action. She stormed across to Rhoda and took her roughly by the shoulders. "Don't try to outguess me, punk," she stabbed harshly, then her eyes snapped up to Mrs. Purdue who stood in the doorway.

"You must go back!" Mrs. Purdue's words were a simple statement of what she believed to be fact.

Lila dropped her hands from Rhoda's shoulders. "How'd you know I was here?"

"Where else would you be? I hear the radio! I see the police cops! I see the bed slept in by two people! Two cigarettes in the ashtray, Rhoda tries to hide. A wastebasket that's got bread and baloney leavings. Wine bottles when my Rhoda don't eat baloney or drink wine." Then with utter contempt she said. "Who else but my Lila who is escaped from prison? Who kills her own father. Who kills a nurse lady who is kind to her. You must go back, Lila, my child."

Rhoda stepped in beside Lila. "Ma, how can you talk like that to your own daughter?"

"THAT you stand next to is no daughter of mine. Ahh, she came joyously from my womb. But the joy has long since turned to pain. It is no daughter of mine who stands here. Only out-and-out tramp I look at."

"And if anybody knows about tramps, it's you, old woman. You ever get around to tellin' Rhoda how you and Pa used to con the merchants for credit? You jazzin' the boy tradesmen and Pa takin' on the..."

Mrs. Purdue's hand lashed viciously across Lila's face to cut off her words. The blow was delivered with such force Lila fell backwards onto the bed.

"You cruddy old bitch!" Lila screamed and

her hand shot under the pillow to come up with a pistol which she levelled directly at her mother's heart. "You cruddy old bitch!" she repeated as she got to her feet. "I've killed for less than that!"

"Sure! You kill! So why not shoot me? One more! Who is to say how much more pain it can cause?"

Rhoda tried to step in between her mother and Lila. "Ma," she said protectingly. "She means it, Ma." And at the same instant, Lila stepped in roughly and pushed her aside.

Mrs. Purdue forced a quick, dry laugh. "Means it? Sure she means it. My Lila, child of my womb, would kill her own ma with no more heart than she did her father." She looked to Rhoda sadly. "And you are with her, Rhoda?"

"You damned well right she's with me. You think she wants to hang around this salami factory all her life?" Lila put the pistol into Rhoda's reluctant hands. "Keep it on the old bitch." Then she turned back to her mother. "Don't get any ideas she won't use it. She ain't got nothin' more to lose now than I have. She helped kill a coupla' guys last night. That makes us good sisters again. She ain't interested in seein' the inside of a prison, and that's just what she'll be doin' if she don't do just like I tell her to do."

Rhoda gasped at the frankness of Lila's words, but she knew they were true. She grabbed the pistol so tightly her knuckles turned white. "I gotta do it this way, Ma!" she said to the stunned woman.

Lila let a pleased smile cross her features, then she took her rope ladder from under the bed, and moved to the window where she secured its hook and tossed the free rope end out into the alley below. When she turned to face Mrs. Purdue and Rhoda again, the smile was gone from her face. In its place was a glare of pure hatred. "Now, old woman, you join the old man. Gimme the gun, Rhoda."

Rhoda's head twitched nervously. She was not at all interested in what Lila had in mind. She fought for time. "People will hear the shot."

Lila leaned over to pick up both bed pillows. "These will muffle the shot." She turned her eyes full on the old woman. "Ain't ya gonna scream so's I can enjoy your last seconds? Come on, old witch, scream for me."

Mrs. Purdue stood steadfast, silent, as her eyes fastened with deep sadness upon what was once her loving child. Rhoda's eyes narrowed as she looked nervously at each of them.

"Gimme the gun," Lila demanded again.

But Rhoda switched the gun so it covered both women. "You're not going to kill her, Lila!" Her voice shook nervously and the crotch of her panties became wet from the sudden, uncontrolled dribble from her kidneys. But she meant business with the gun.

"Are you outta' your mind?"

"Get outta' the window. Ma's stayin' here so you got time to get away."

"I can't take off until tonight. You know that."

150

Rhoda shrugged. "You're not killin' Ma. Now beat it! Beat it while you got time. And Ma, I don't want to hurt you. Don't do anything to make me hurt you."

"Punk, you're as flaky as that tit eater, Babs. The minute you turn her loose she's gonna call the fuzz. You're gonna be in the lock-up right alongside of me."

"Ma won't say nothin'!" she snapped. "Now beat it!"

"What about tonight? The boat..." She caught herself. "The both of us? Our plans?"

"Take off!" Rhoda's hands shook nervously. She was frightened but determined, and although Lila might at another time have tried to take the girl, the nervous trigger finger forced her to back down. She went to the window and climbed out.

Rhoda waited until Lila was gone before she spoke to the statue-like figure of her mother. "Is she sayin' the truth, Ma? You won't talk to the cops? Not until tomorrow? Give us time to get away?"

"Give me that gun, Rhoda!"

"I can't... not now, Ma."

"GIVE ME THAT GUN!"

"Ma," she pleaded. "Ma. Listen to me... you don't have to turn us in. You don't have to say Lila was here. Let her go. It can't hurt you none... no more. It can't hurt you to let her go."

The sadness overwhelmed Mrs. Purdue's voice. She felt older than her years. Her entire life had collapsed before her eyes in a matter of moments.

"Can't hurt me anymore." The tears twinkled in her tired old eyes. "Can't hurt me anymore…" Then her voice rose to a screaming pitch. "How soon you have forgotten. LILA KILLED YOUR FATHER!" And with that outburst, Mrs Purdue dived at the gun. Both her hands gripped Rhoda's hand which held the death-dealing instrument. But her move had been all wrong for safety. She had pulled the gun toward her and the muffled explosion came as the barrel embedded itself into her stomach flesh.

Mrs. Purdue's eyes held a startled expression as a whisp of smoke drifted up across her face. She winced against the sudden, searing pain. Her eyes closed and she slipped silently to the floor.

Rhoda stood transfixed for another long moment as she held the gun limply in her hand. She let the instrument fall to the floor beside the old woman, then in a state of shock Rhoda bent down, over her.

"Ma! Ma! I didn't mean it." She looked horrified to the life-giving red fluid as it pumped out of her mother's stomach. Then panic took over reason. Rhoda got up and raced out of the room.

Mrs. Purdue's eyes fluttered open a few minutes later. She fought her mind out of her own state of shock and gripping her stomach tightly with one hand, she staggered to her feet, then made her way to the door.

CHAPTER FOURTEEN

Reverend Steele had conducted the late afternoon graveside services for Amos Hemp, then, mentally weary from the events of the past few days, he decided a walk in the early evening air might quiet his nerves. He'd had a few ideas he wanted to talk over with Sheriff Buck Rhodes, but the lawman had been away from his usual haunts all day. Sometime during the afternoon he'd visited Miss O'Hara at the hospital. The poor woman was in a horrible condition but the blessings of unconsciousness were merciful to her in relieving her of pain. There would be a surgeon somewhere in the world who, in time, could make her face once more presentable. It would take time.

There was little he could do for the two boys. Not enough left of them for the undertaker to work with. There could only be the few words over closed caskets as he had just done for Mr. Hemp who had no face. Narcotics had strange rewards.

He moved on until the saloons were more frequent and the smells more plentiful. Then in the deep shadows of an alley, across from the Purdue delicatessen, he saw Herb Tyler's car, so he walked to it.

"Still at it, I see, Herb."

Herb nodded his head. "Thought you'd be tied up on old Amos' funeral half the night."

"Because of the body's condition and the incident itself, the family decided not to hold a wake.

I admit I advised it, but it is much better this way."

"Our little town's become a hellion, Hank."

"So it would appear. Have you heard from Buck lately?"

"Yeah. He's back at the office. Called me a while back. Told me to stay on here until he could send over a relief man. He left Harry, my regular, out at the mine cabin for the night. Doesn't want anybody nosing around until he can finish up the investigation in the daylight. You want to talk with him?" Herb indicated his car radio.

"I did earlier. It'll wait. He has more important things on his mind just now, I'm sure." Reverend Steele looked across to the delicatessen. "Lila would be a fool to come back here."

"And I'd say you're right. Just the younger kid and folks buying things. That's the way it's been yesterday and today. Say, you know, if I had a daughter that stayed out like that kid, cussin' the way she does, I'd kick her ass all over the sidewalk, not just slap her across the puss once."

Reverend Steele flushed. "You saw that, huh?"

"Couldn't help it. I don't know how you took her sass as long as you did." Then before he could add to his observations, he looked directly through the windshield, across to the delicatessen. "The old lady looks like she's coming out."

The clergyman looked across the street. "Excuse me, Herb," and he moved out quickly to confront Mrs. Purdue as she turned the key in the

154

delicatessen front door with her right hand. Her left hand clutched her side tightly, over a heavy coat she had put on to cover the blood.

"Good evening, Mrs. Purdue," Reverend Steele greeted, tipping his hat.

Mrs. Purdue gave the clergyman a brief, saddened look, then without speaking she turned and went off down the street, staggering into the darkness. Reverend Steele thought about going after her for a moment, but after she had gone around the far corner, he changed his mind and recrossed the street to Herb's car. "Get Buck on that thing, Herb."

Buck's car sped into the dirty street with siren blaring moments after he received Steele's call for assistance. The inhabitants of the street scurried from their holes like lice from a beaten mattress. Their eyes watched nervously as Buck swung quickly out of his side door and Reverend Steele, with Herb, crossed to join him. "What do you think it's all about Hank?"

"I don't know, Buck. That's why I thought you'd better get out here. There's something mighty wrong when Mrs. Purdue acts as she did. She looked bad, real bad, Buck. Staggered off that way," he pointed to the corner.

"No tellin' which way she went once she got 'round that there corner." He turned to look to the store. "Let's take a look inside."

"She's locked the door."

"I got a pass key for every joint in the town. Come on!"

Herb put his hand lightly on Buck's shoulder. "How about a search warrant? Nothing wrong... old lady Purdue can get mighty huffy. She might not like us going in there."

"When's a search warrant ever stopped me from doing what I set out to do Herb? Come on!"

Herb shrugged, then with Reverend Steele, he followed Buck to his car where he took out a pass key, then the three men made their way to the delicatessen and entered.

The bright lights inside reflected against fresh blood spots on the floor as they trailed toward the stairway. Buck leaned over and scraped his finger lightly across the sticky fluid. "Blood alright," he remarked. Then he stood up and looked to the back stairway. They started for it.

Rhoda's room proved their suspicions. Buck picked up the pistol with a handkerchief and handed it to Herb who carefully secreted it into his pocket.

"Somebody's been hurt badly," clucked the reverend, "and it's my guess that somebody was Mrs. Purdue."

"If it is," sighed Buck, "she's runnin' mighty low on blood, judgin' from the size of that spot there."

Herb walked the window, attracted by the hook affixed there. "What's this thing?" He pulled up the rope ladder.

Buck crossed to take the knotted rope in his hand. "Unless I miss my guess, that's the way Lila has been getting in and out of this room so unseen. The alley is blocked on the street side and ties into a building on the next street. She goes through a door or windows in the building, then who can tell how she winds her way back to the streets, or the desert."

"She said if she ever got the chance she'd get even with the old lady," reflected Herb.

"And chances are nobody heard the shot or it would have been reported by now," determined Buck.

"No one but Mrs. Purdue and those in the room," said Reverend Sleele.

"Couldn't have been the young girl," remembered Herb. "She lit out of here more than half an hour ago. I got the exact time on my notes in the car."

"Herb," ordered Buck. "Get on your radio. Have my deputy Bob cruise the south part of town. And have him tell Doc Gibbons to stand by in case I need him right quick."

Herb silently turned on his heels and walked quickly out of the room.

"Buck," said Reverend Steele when Herb was gone. "It hit me last night the same as it has hit me tonight. I'm talking about the lack of juveniles, especially the girls, on the street tonight. They were gone last night, and we know now what happened. Tonight is beginning to hold the same feeling, the same atmosphere."

"I hadn't noticed it, but then I haven't been on the streets all day. But, we're not doing any good up here. Let's go down and have a look around.

I saw Jockey in the crowd when we came up, and if anybody knows anything about anything, it will be Jockey."

Jockey and Chief were standing just outside the front door of the delicatessen as Buck and Reverend Steele approached them. "Is somebody hurt?" asked Jockey, honestly concerned.

"It is possible," reflected Reverend Steele.

"Jockey, do you get the feelin' all ain't right on the street tonight?" questioned Buck as he lit a cigar.

Jockey nodded his head. "Same's last night, Sheriff. The kids are gone again."

"Then you have noticed it." stated Reverend Steele.

"Who could help it?"

Buck let a cloud of smoke trail off into the breeze. "Any rumbles of what they might be up to?"

He shook his head. "I guess I'm usually the first to grab onto a rumble, Sheriff, but I ain't heard one word on this one, or the one last night, if that's what it was. You can bet one thing. It's too quiet tonight for a healthy climate."

Buck and the Reverend turned to walk off as Chief drew Jockey out of earshot of the crowd.

"Party," uttered the giant Indian.

Jockey looked to his cook with deep concern. "You hear somethin' Chief?"

The big man shrugged his broad shoulders. "Don't know what good I hear. Hear girl get in jalopy, tell boy must get back quick. Party on

158

boat. Tonight. No boys."

Jockey's face became elated. He snapped his fingers as realization gained a foothold in his brain. "You got it, Chief... Lark... that lousy crumbum bastard Lark. Come on! We gotta find the boat he came in on."

"You think lousy crumbum bastard Lark come here on boat?"

"How else do you suppose he brings in that stuff he peddles? It don't swim in from down Mexico way."

"We'll get the cops!"

"First we make sure," said Jockey, and started off quickly down the street, with Chief following, in the direction of the docks beyond the red-light district. Momentarily it appeared Chief would stop when they passed Buck and Reverend Steele at the police car, but he continued on as Jockey had previously directed.

"We're reasonably sure Lila is in the area," said the sheriff. "And we know she used to be leader of the Chicks before she got sent up. And all the Chicks have took off for the tall timbers tonight..."

"I'd hazard a guess, Buck, that Mrs. Purdue may have found out their plans. Lila wouldn't have risked a shot in that old barn they call home, unless she was forced into it."

"Well, let's figure it out, padre. What would be such an important plan as to risk that shot!" Buck's words had not formed a question. "So we can put a few things together. Miss Long was killed because she overheard about a shipment of dope. Miss O'Hara is in bad shape because, at least on the face of it, she caught a coupla' boys puffin' pot on the school grounds. Probably Lonnie and Rick from her earlier description. Then Lonnie and Rick are blown to bits with what they thought was their fix candle..."

"I didn't know that, Buck!" interrupted the Reverend in complete surprise.

"Nobody does. Except we cops and the killer. Anyway, it all leads to one thing..."

"Dope," said Reverend Steele knowingly.

"Right! Now we know it was meant to come up the coast by boat. But what boat? And what in hell have the kids to do with it, and more than that, where does Lila fit in, since she only got out of prison two nights ago?"

"Perhaps it is as you indicated before. Once, she was the leader of the Chicks, and it is a good possibility the Chicks are going to have something to do with transporting the stuff. Rhoda is a Chick. It wouldn't be very hard for Lila to get anything out of Rhoda she wanted. I found out, last night, for certain, that Rhoda is a user."

"I guessed as much." He turned to look off in the direction of the Gulf, which could not be seen from where they stood. "But how to find out? There's a lot of water out there. A million places for a small boat to row into and get away. It would take us days to search every boat, even if they did have a gang of kids on it. They won't be yellin' and screamin' to let us know just where they're at.

And if we did hear some party sounds I'd bet you another five to one they'd be decoys on trespassed boats."

"I've got an idea."

"Spill it, Hank."

"Can you arrange for me to see Jenny again? Right now?"

"It's pretty late, but—sure I can arrange it. What have you got in mind?"

"Just a hunch so far."

"And I'm gettin' your hunch. She was a Chick?"

"She's on the stuff."

"You sure?"

"Certain. That morning she was still on the effects. But it wore off. Doc Gibbons told me this afternoon at the hospital that he had to fix her up this morning." He paused briefly. "And she showed me her arm marks."

"Why wasn't I told?"

"You've been out all day."

"Yeah! Yeah, that's right. Okay, I'll fix it up, but this time I go with you."

"Of course." Then he got a twinkle in his eye. "But why don't you let me talk to her first? We got along quite well before, and I might be able to promise her a few things you couldn't, and you wouldn't be held accountable for."

"That ain't honest, Reverend."

"Dope isn't honest either," said Reverend Steele solidly.

The two men got into the police car and while they drove to the court-house Buck put in his radio call to Judge Detler, who gave permission for the interview but also cautioned Buck that anything she said could not be used as evidence against the girl unless her lawyer was present. Since Jenny had no lawyer and would most probably fall a burden of the state with the expense of a public defender, Buck said "Okay Judge. We'll work it this way. Reverend Steele will make the interview and I'll stay out of it altogether."

When Buck hung up the radio-phone he looked back to his friend. "Okay Hank, it's your show again."

Jenny was sleepy-eyed as old Rance brought her into the room, then departed again. "What you want with me? I was sleepin'."

"Very early for that, Jenny."

"Might be on the outside. But in here, ain't nothin' to do but sleep. What you want anyway?"

"I want to know what the Chicks had on for tonight."

"Clothes," she snapped, then laughed.

"Make it easier or tougher on yourself."

"How the hell do I know? I'm in here. They're outside."

Reverend Steele started to get up from his chair. "Okay, have it your way Jenny."

She thought it over quickly. "Easier, you say?"

"Cooperation always makes things go easier in a courtroom."

"You promise?"

"I promise to help you as much as I can."

"Alright... but it ain't a whole lot."

A few minutes later, Reverend Steele joined Buck in the squad car outside the court-house. "What'd you find out?" asked Buck anxiously.

"Some things, but not enough. First of all, remember back to the fall and winter when you had that epidemic of shoplifting on your hands. It was the Chicks. They have specially built clothing for handling merchandise. Hidden pockets and seams that aren't seams, things like that. Double skirts and hollow falsies..."

"And those hidden elements are so easily converted to the purpose of carrying narcotics..."

"Right. They pick it up usually at some innocent enough appearing teenage party, such as on a boat, the girls fill their clothing and bring it ashore to a dump. Who would suspect a bunch of teenagers, especially girls, leaving a party to be transporters of a major supply of narcotics? The boat, this time, is mostly my idea. Jenny didn't know anything except that a boat was supposed to be on the way and it had been done that way before. But whose boat or where, she didn't know. She couldn't know anything about tonight's action because she's been in jail almost since the action started."

"It only proved out our suspicions. What'd you promise her for the information?"

"That things would go easier for her."

"That will be hard to make come true. There's only one punishment for murder handed out by Judge Gibbons."

"She wasn't worried about court or her punishment. She wanted to make sure it would be easier for her while she waited... I'll have to send Doc Gibbons over to see her."

CHAPTER FIFTEEN

Jockey and Chief hid in the shadows of a warehouse on the dock as they looked out over the dark waters of the Gulf beyond. There were many well-lighted yachts in the harbor; some big, some small, and some form of music issued from nearly all of them.

"Hard to find," muttered Chief.

"Ain't gonna be easy. But I know what his boat looks like. All we gotta do is get close enough so's I can lamp it."

"How do we do that?"

"Swim if we have to."

"No swim! Me desert Indian, not water Indian."

Jockey laughed lightly. "Guess we'll have to find a boat in that case."

"Where?"

"Some of the guys always tie up at the end of the pier when they come into town. Wouldn't surprise me none if we find what we want right there."

"Ugh," muttered Chief harshly, then followed Jockey's footsteps, keeping in the deep shadows, towards the end of the pier.

It was as Jockey had surmised. Several small dinghies with outboard motors were tied to various pilings below the pier. He motioned for Chief to wait where he was, then climbed down a rickety ladder to the water level catwalk. For some minutes he went about opening gas tanks and testing the level of gas in them. Finally he was satisfied when he withdrew a completely wet forefinger from one. "I got a full one," he called in a harsh whisper to the chief. "Come on down."

The ladder nearly gave way under Chief's excessive weight as he descended, but the water level catwalk had enough spring to give with the weight. Chief made sure, however, of his footing with each step he took, until he stood near Jockey, who was trying to untie a knot in the fat mooring rope. Chief, quickly sensing the little man's problem, took the rope in both hands and with one quick jerk, tore the hemp in two. Jockey gave him a pat on the back approvingly, then got into the boat and moved to the outboard motor in the stern where he started adjusting the lanyard around the motor wheel.

Chief looked to the skimpy boat, then took much more care in getting into it, and even so, his weight sunk the gunnels dangerously close to the water line. He eased his way to the center seat so that the boat was more evenly distributed around him.

Jockey had felt sure they were both in for a cold saltwater bath when he saw the bow dip, but he breathed easier as the boat levelled off with Chief in the middle and sitting, frightened, frozen to the spot. The little man grabbed the lanyard tightly and gave it a swift, snapping pull. The motor exploded into sudden life and the dark waters churned up under the keel and the propeller. Satisfied the motor was delivering properly, he turned the bow toward the yachts and fishing boats far out in the harbor, where nestled among a group of fishing boats rested the solid black trawler, The Phantom.

Lark had named his boat well. Its dull ebony finish could glide by coastguard vessels within a few hundred yards at night and not be seen. Many were the times it had appeared on radar screens, yet could not be seen with the naked eye or telescope; it blended so well with the black waters and moonless nights. By the same token, Lark never made narco trips during moonlit nights. On such nights, the black Phantom stood out as a giant bird of prey against the lighter sky.

Throughout the evening Lark had been nervous due to the gang's uncalled-for activities. If it hadn't been for the fact he had already designated to his superiors where and when the drop would be, he would have called off the whole thing, hoisted anchor and sailed elsewhere along the coast. But he was also fearful his superiors would get the impression he couldn't handle his end of things— a bunch of snotty-nosed kids.

His eyes pressed across the fan tail towards the shore line for a time, then he would change their direction towards the open sea and back again. Over and over he repeated the operation. If a ship, large or small, came anywhere close to his position, he tensed up and came forward in his chair, his hand hanging close to the deck beside him where he had a submachine gun loaded and ready for use. He would settle back when the boat had gone, but the tension never completely left him. All his orders were carried out through his second, Claude, who made frequent trips to the bridge to report or to get further orders.

Around ten-thirty, Claude made his way up the ship's ladder in an angry mood. "Boss, that sister of Lila's ain't cooperatin' one damned bit."

Lark looked to the man with hard eyes. "What's the matter with her?"

"Who knows? Can't even get her to talk. She just sits around sulkin'. Words go in one ear and out the other like she don't give a goddamn about nothin'."

"Okay. Send Lila up here." Claude started off but stopped as Lark called him back. "And get your wet suit on. I'm sendin' you down now."

Claude looked to his wristwatch. "It's only ten-thirty. You ain't figurin' on gettin' the stuff 'til midnight."

"So I changed my mind."

"So I get ready." Claude shrugged and left the bridge.

Below decks he found Lila sitting alone in the small kitchen with a double shot of whiskey in front of her. "You and that sister of yours have a fight?"

"What's it to you?"

"Boss don't like it."

"She's damned lucky I haven't tossed her over the side."

"Boss don't want no trouble aboard. He wants to see you, and right now."

Lila slugged down the whiskey then walked

slowly through the short corridor, then climbed to the deck. She looked up to Lark on the bridge above her. "You want me?"

"Come up here. I don't want to be shouting all over the harbor."

Lila took hold of the ladder and climbed up. A moment later she stood beside Lark. "So?"

"What's eating your sister?"

"She's got troubles. Me!"

"I don't want trouble aboard my ship."

"There won't be any. Only reason she's here is because she ain't got no place else to go. The old lady knows she was in on the kill last night."

"And the old lady will squawk on her as she did you?"

"Sure. Only I'm going to Mexico with you. She finds her own way out of town. When I give an order I want it obeyed, no matter who it is."

"You're a rough one, Lila."

"I told her to lay the old lady out. She turned the gun on me."

"Well look. I need her to carry some of the stuff ashore. Leave her in one piece until after that, then I don't care what you do with her."

"Sure," said Lila coldly.

"Soon's you talk to her, get your girls ready. I'm pushing the drop forward. Claude's gone to get the stuff now."

"Where is it?"

"I've got a false keel in the bow. It's all in waterproof bags in the keel." He beamed in pride.

"Claude will bring it up."

Lila nodded her approval and went down the ladder again to the deck where she encountered two of her girls looking out over the water toward the dark horizon. "Either of you see Rhoda?"

The girls turned toward her as one said. "Yeah, she went into the toilet on the starboard side."

Lila slapped the girl a vicious blow across the mouth. "That's for bein' a wiseguy." And she stormed off along the starboard deck while the girl frantically rubbed the pain from the side of her face.

As Lila put her hand out to grab the knob, Rhoda pushed open the head door from the inside. "I've been lookin' for you, punk," said Lila.

"You want to kill me?"

"I ain't got time. Look, Lark don't like the way you been actin'. So now pull yourself together. You got a job to do, and by Christ I'm gonna see that you do it."

"Take me with you, Lila. Take me to Mexico with you."

"Are you kiddin'? It's only lucky Lark is takin' me. You beat it on back. Maybe Ma won't turn you in."

"She don't have to. I shot Ma!"

The surprise of the statement rocked Lila. "You did what?"

"Just after you left. I shot Ma!" The tears came to her eyes quickly. "I shot her dead."

170

Lila took a marijuana cigarette and a match from her pocket. She put it between her sister's lips. "For that, maybe even I can forgive you. Here. Take some of this." She held the match out for the younger girl to light up.

Rhoda lit up and breathed deeply. "It was an accident. Just after you left she dived for me. We fought a little and the gun went off. She went down. Blood all over her. I didn't mean it. But I did it. She just laid there on the floor near the bed. She was so still. I knew she was dead right there and then."

Lila grinned. "I knew you wouldn't let me down. Accident or no accident. Guess that really makes us sisters again. Two of a kind, we are. I did in the old man and now you lay out the old lady."

"How can you be so cold about it?"

"How else should I be? I wanted to do it all along. I'll even forget you turning the gun on me. I'll always wonder if you really would have used it on me. And maybe you would. You're a killer now, and a killer has to kill." She took the weed from Rhoda's lips and inhaled deeply herself, then put it back between Rhoda's lips again. "Well, it's done. Why worry ourselves into an early grave alongside of them? Besides, what in hell good were they? What did they ever do for us except feed us tons of salami? Give either of them another fifty years and what could they have done for us? You damned well know what." She let a broad grin pass across her

171

features. "I think we did them a big favor by puttin' them out of their misery."

Rhoda wiped the tears onto the arm of her cashmere sweater. "Maybe that's the way you think, Lila. But something inside of me hurts... hurts bad..."

Lila indicated the marijuana cigarette in Rhoda's free hand. "Take another blast off that thing. You'll lose all your hurts in a coupla' minutes. In fact, take a couple of real quick blasts. That makes things seem not so bad even quicker." She turned to the open deck again. "Wait here where I can find you. I gotta tell Lark that everything's alright." Then she made her way back midship again.

CHAPTER SIXTEEN

Jockey cut his motor some distance from The Phantom as soon as he recognized the trawler as the quarry for which he looked. Chief still hung on to the gunnels for dear life, still frightened of making the slightest move and turning over the boat. However, as the motor died, he ventured to turn his head slightly in Jockey's direction. "Gas gone?"

"No Chief. And keep your voice down. Sound carries a long way over water. I cut the motor off for that reason. We're gonna sneak up on that bunch. Maybe that way we got a chance of not gettin' shot at."

"How boat go no gas motor?"

"Arm power! See them oars by your feet?"

Chief looked down toward his feet. "Oars?"

"Them long heavy sticks!"

"Uh! Chief see."

"Well, put them in the locks there on each side of the boat and row."

"Like canoe?"

"That's right. And don't splash the water any more than you have to. We want to make like quiet... all quiet..."

"Chief know."

A moment later, Jockey found to his pleasant surprise Chief handled the oars like an expert. The small boat cut the black waters smoothly and silently. "Head for the bow, Chief."

"Where that?"

Jockey pointed. "Up that way. Where the anchor chain is."

Chief nodded. "Okay! No talk no more. Too close!"

Jockey smiled appreciatively, then kept his eyes steadfast on The Phantom. He could make out two dark figures on the bridge but couldn't tell who they were. However, since it was the bridge, he surmised one was Lark. He cursed the man under his breath. He knew he could immediately turn his little dinghy around and head for shore and the police, but the excitement of the chase caressed his better judgment into submission. The courage of a James Bond filled his entire frame. He could read future headlines bigger than he'd ever gotten for the races he had ridden and won. If only he could capture the smugglers single-handed; with Chief of course. "Bare hands against tommy guns," he mused to himself, pleased with himself.

He remained thus engrossed as Chief reached up to grab the anchor chain as their dinghy passed under it. Jockey shook his head to lose the daydream, but not the spirit of adventure. As silent as a cat he climbed hand over hand up the anchor chain until he planted his feet firmly on a small portion of the deck which extended beyond the guard rail. The little man ducked down behind the guard rail and siding as he watched Chief, belying his weight, climb the anchor chain with as much ease as he himself had done. But the deck extension was nowhere near wide enough to sup-

174

port Chief. The big Indian used it only to hoist himself over the railing. Jockey followed immediately after him, then they both froze in their tracks as they looked down the muzzle of Claude's pistol.

"Lookin' for more plate-glass windows?" he said.

Chief's big hands and arms went up over his head. He growled and was about to charge both man and gun, but Jockey put a heavy hand on his wide girth. "Not now, Chief. It ain't worth gettin' shot up for."

"Now that's real smart of you, little man."

"You should be so smart."

Claude laughed cynically at Jockey, then without turning his head in that direction, he shouted to Lark. "Hey, Lark!"

Lark, on the bridge, turned in his chair. "What do you want, Claude?" He could not see the action behind him, at the bow.

"Look what came out of the water with me."

Lark looked lazily at Lila. "See what in hell's goin' on down there."

Lila moved to the bridge railing and looked to the bow, then she turned back to the man. "You better have a look. We got unexpected visitors aboard."

Lark got out of his chair and went to join Lila. His eyes opened wide at what he saw. "Keep that gun on them. I'll be right down."

"They ain't goin' no place," shouted Claude.

Lark turned to Lila. "Keep an eye on the shore-

175

line and the docks. You see lights of any kind, automobile, boats, even more dock lights than what's on now, let me know."

"Sure, Lark."

Lark swiftly climbed down to the deck and made his way to the bow where he stood next to Claude. "I saw their boat above me when I was comin' up with the stuff, so I came up on the other side and waited for them."

"That's good work."

Claude narrowed his eyes. "I wonder who is gonna throw who out a window this time."

Chief growled. "I show."

Jockey again put a restrained hand on Chief's belly. "Hold it, Chief. We ain't got no window out here."

"Bright boy's got a sense of humor," sneered Claude. He cocked the pistol. "Say your prayers."

"Not here. Not yet," said Lark. Then he put his hands defiantly on his hips. "First, you don't like the idea of joining my business venture. Then here you are crashing a private party on my private property. What's with you, Jockey? You got holes in your head since you retired?"

"He WILL have holes in his head," informed Claude.

"You got a lot of witnesses round here tonight," said Jockey factually.

"Embarrassed at dying in front of an audience? From what I remember of your race days, you ought to be able to do a real good performance."

"Witnesses are witnesses," smiled Jockey, but the smile was not one of pleasure.

Lark frowned. "Hate to admit you're right, but you are."

Claude snapped his eyes to Lark. "You ain't thinkin' of lettin' them go?"

"That would be silly, wouldn't it Claude? Act your age."

"Then what do we do with them?"

Lark began to pace back and forth behind Claude so that he did not interfere with Claude's aim. When he had a plan in mind he stopped pacing and looked directly at the two captives. "First of all, it would take too much time to get all the kids off the ship in the little boat. Too many trips back and forth. I'm going to chance taking this tub to the dock, get the kids off and head out into the Gulf just as fast as we can make it."

"The fuzz'll grab us for sure."

"If they were onto us, they'd be here now. My guess is Jockey hit onto a lucky guess. He knew my boat from a long time ago. But there isn't any telling how long it will be before something else does give the cops a hint. I want that stuff ashore. It's our necks if it isn't at the drop tonight. We make one dash in, get the girls off and get out of there."

Claude wiggled the gun at Jockey and Chief. "What's to keep them from makin' a break for it once we're on the dock?"

Lark directed his gaze at Jockey. "Two very

good reasons. If we start shooting, a stray bullet might hit one of those girls. And the other, I'd gun them down before they could move a foot. It's human nature to want to live as long as possible. In their minds will always be the thought of a possible escape. The longer they are alive, the more chance they think they will have. I think the kids are the best reason they won't try it, however. Jockey wouldn't want any of them hurt—now would you Jockey?"

"You're holdin' the pat hand," replied Jockey. "This deal anyway."

"Glad you see it my way Jockey, since this is the only time we're dealing in this game." He turned away, but before going he snapped his last words to Claude. "Keep your gun on them and don't waste time talking if they make a funny move."

"They ain't going no place." And as Lark moved back along the deck toward the bridge ladder, Claude once more moved the pistol menacingly at his captives. "Why don't you two sit down on the anchor rope there where I can watch you better? Besides, you'll be more comfortable. It's quite a way back to the dock."

"Chief know—Chief rowed," grunted the big Indian as he squatted down beside Jockey on the anchor rope.

Lark walked across the bridge and entered the wheel house where he snapped on the ignition. He listened for the motors to purr into being, then looked to Lila who had followed him inside.

178

"Get your girls loaded up. Claude's got the stuff in the bow. I want them loaded and ready to jump ashore the second I hit the dock. I don't want any waiting around or delays."

"You're taking The Phantom in?" she asked, her voice a high-pitched entity of surprise, "Stop asking fool questions and do as you're told. You got just about nine minutes to load up and have the girls at the starboard rail."

Without another word, Lila raced out of the wheel house and Lark pressed a lever marked "ANCHOR".

Claude bellowed in hysterical glee as the anchor rope pulling the chair moved suddenly under Jockey and Chief. Both men fell flat on their faces on the deck.

CHAPTER SEVENTEEN

Lila, with Dee's help, had the narcotics spilled from their waterproof coverings and spread out on the galley table before the other girls arrived on the scene. It was the largest haul any of them had ever seen, and Babs remarked about it as her eyes bugged at the array of pills, glassine-enclosed powders and small, flat bricks of pressed marijuana. "Man," she said. "If this ain't a junkie's paradise."

"That's more'n a million bucks you're lookin' at, fruitcake," jeered Lila. "So get it in your girdle and make it quick. You ain't got much time." Lila concluded her orders at the galley entrance, then went out as the girls began to strip off their outer clothing.

Hollow, foam rubber falsies received their share of narcotic padding. Girdles with built-up sides and fannies, also of hollow foam rubber with hidden accesses were soon stuffed to capacity. Small plastic vials found their way into the vagina and rectum. Smaller glassine packets were glued under false finger- and toenails. Smooth arms and legs suddenly developed ugly theatrical make-up scars which could hide a pill or two.

Dee loaded up quickly, then, as she buttoned her sweater, she looked across to Rhoda who, fully dressed, made her way through the galley door as she headed for the deck. Surprised that anyone could have beaten her in loading up and getting dressed since she had started first, she went

went out after the girl. Rhoda leaned over the railing looking toward the dock which was gettting closer with each passing moment when Dee leaned in beside her. "You must be in a hurry to load up that fast."

Rhoda did not look to her. "I didn't take any."

"Lila will kill you!"

"So she'll kill me!"

"Well, look at it another way. Think of all the loot."

"I'm not sure I want any of it... now."

"You gotta be crazy."

"It doesn't seem important anymore." Her eyes held a vacant stare which bothered Dee. They appeared to be looking but not seeing anything. "I didn't think I'd ever want anything more than I did gold—and good times—and excitement. I guess I lived it day and night. Gold! Bread! Loot! I quit school to get it. Money was the only thing that was important in the whole world to me and I didn't care much how I got it. And I liked it so's I could buy fly juice and powder! Pot! Hashish! Now it's all changed. I don't want any of it. Why fly when there's no place left to fly?"

Dee shrugged broadly. "You know what I think? I think you're loony. I think you've flipped your everlovin' wig. I never heard such a thing. Don't like bread? You better not let your sister hear you talkin' that way."

"Just leave me alone, will you Dee?"

Dec's eyes hardened. "That's the way you want it? Okay! But don't cry to me when Lila feeds your tits to Babs." The girl walked off toward the fan tail where several of the other girls had already started to gather for their quick disembarkation.

Although Chief still faced Claude and his gun, Jockey looked out over the bow railing to the dock. The lights seemed to be coming toward them instead of the other way around. Claude beamed self-confidently. "Don't let the sight of dry land throw you, boys. We'll be out to sea again in a few minutes."

"I can hardly wait," muttered Jockey without turning around.

Claude moved a step closer to Chief and prodded him a few times with the muzzle of his gun. "You know how I'm going to give it to you, big shit?" He watched the Indian's eyes and saw no change in them. "Slow! Real slow! I want you should see the fishes that's gonna eat your insides for a long time before you die. I owe you plenty for that beatin' you give me the other night. I only wish I had a window I could throw you through before you hit the water down there." He stepped back again to his original position a few paces from Chief. "Now sit down behind the rail guard so you can't be seen from the other side."

Jockey turned on Claude as Chief did as he was told. "You better lay off him. He might get real mad."

Claude tapped his gun with his left hand. "This

182

makes me as big as him. Maybe even bigger."

"What makes you think one little bullet can stop a big hulk of an Indian like him?"

"I'm an excellent shot," bragged Claude.

"So was General Custer," grinned Jockey.

Rhoda stood in the shadows just below the wheel house but she could see Claude and the others quite clearly. She didn't like to see Jockey hurt, but there wasn't much she could do about it. She felt alone, against everyone else, and she felt even more alone as Lark maneuvered the trawler's starboard side into the dock, with the bow facing toward the open sea in case he had to make the sudden getaway he felt he was ready for.

Having been given their orders, and told that there would not be time to tie up, the girls began jumping to the dock as soon as the boat hit it.

Lark kept the starboard side hitting the piling with all the pressure his motors could afford. He didn't want any of the girls slipping into the water where he would lose any of the stuff, and as the last one jumped to the dock he turned to Lila. "Now you get ashore."

Lila's mouth fell open. "I thought I was going across the border with you... you said..."

Lark cut her off. "That don't go any more, broad. You and your crazy sister have been enough trouble. How long you think it's going to take them to find out it was you two who did in Lonnie and Rick? Beat it. And if you know what's good for you, you'll keep your mouth shut.

I've got friends inside prison as well as outside. Maybe the judge won't give you the big black, but one of my friends and a shiv will. You couldn't prove nothin' against me anyway. Just cause me a lot of trouble. There's no room for PIGS in the BIG TIME!"

"They'll grab me."

"That's your problem. Get going." And he slapped her a sharp crack across the face which sent her out of the door and to the bridge railing.

As she came away from the railing, rubbing her arm where it had cracked against the railing, she glared at the man in the wheel house with all the hatred she possessed. "Oh brother! Bastard, are YOU going to be sorry you did that!" She moved off toward the bridge ladder. "I once said... only once."

Unseen by the others, Rhoda slipped over the side and into a dark spot on the dock near a thick set of pilings. It was easy for her to grab up a mooring rope which dangled over the starboard side of the trawler, and she fastened it to an iron dock link. The boat was at least temporarily secured to the dock.

Lark shifted into forward gear and pressed the accelerator lever forward. The boat shot out to the end of the line, then snapped to a dead stop. Lark slid to the deck near the wheel.

Claude lost his footing and fell into the arms of the seated Indian. The giant arms went around the man like giant boa constrictors. Claude's back snapped before he could utter a sound.

In the same jerking action, Lila tumbled forward and slid over the gun Claude had dropped. She quickly grabbed up the gun and disappeared back under the wheel house just as the floodlight from the dock covered the entire ship, and Sheriff Buck Rhodes' voice came over a bull-horn. "You on the boat! All of you! Put your hands up and come ashore."

"Claude," screamed Lark from the deck of the wheel house. His leg was broken. "Claude, for Christ's sake cut that rope... Claude!"

"He's dead," said Lila from the doorway, and she fired the pistol. The bullet went straight into his left eye.

Lark died without a sound. Only a look of terror.

But the sound of the shot brought a volley from the police on the pier. Lila ducked down behind the bridge guard, then made her way down the ladder. She belly-crawled along the deck until she found a dark spot near the stern, then she climbed over the side and came up behind Rhoda. She locked her strong left arm around the younger girl's neck.

"We've got all the girls. The rest of you come out," shouted Buck's voice over the bull-horn again.

"You just stay back. I'm comin' through your lines, or my sister gets it!" screamed Lila, and the searchlights were turned on her. She held Rhoda securely around the neck with her left arm, and the pistol ready for instant action with the right.

"Put that girl down," ordered Buck.

"Lila," came the voice of Reverend Steele as he stepped up beside Buck. "This is not the way."

"You get back, preacher, or you'll be meetin' that Lord you're always talkin' about before you grow another minute older."

"She means what she says!" The voice from the darkness, hoarse and weak, caused the lawmen and Reverend Steele to look around. Mrs. Purdue, clutching her side where the blood had soaked through her coat, came out of the darkness.

"Ma!" screamed Rhoda in utter disbelief.

Lila pulled Rhoda back through an opening in the guard railing so that they stood on the deck of the trawler again as Mrs. Purdue, some few feet ahead of the police, walked toward them. "When my Lila shot her own father she was signing a death warrant for anybody she would ever point a gun at again!"

"Shut up!" screamed Lila and fired a shot into the planking in front of the old woman. But Mrs. Purdue didn't blink an eye. She moved forward. "Keep her back, or I swear I'll gun her down where she stands."

"Please, Mrs. Purdue. Wait!" pleaded Reverend Steele.

The voice caused the old woman to stop momentarily, only a few steps from the girls. She looked back to the Reverend. "I have little time for waiting," she spluttered, then coughed bitterly.

"We'd better humor Lila," whispered Reverend Steele to Buck.

"Yeah. Maybe we can get the other girl. If she gets to sea, she can't get far. We'll have the coast-guard on it in minutes." Then he raised his voice. "Okay, Lila. You let the others go and we won't stop you from getting away. Just let the others go."

"I feel safer this way. My sister and those jerks go with me." She indicated Jockey and Chief who had remained in the bow. "Jockey and Chief get it first in case of trouble. My sister respects me," she beamed but did not lessen her hold on Rhoda's neck. "We'll beat this rap yet, kid. You and me together. Just you and me, all the way." Lila's mind began to jump.

"I don't want to go with you, Lila," sobbed Rhoda.

"Sure you do. Say, who's been gettin' through to you? If I thought it was that Holy Joe up there…"

"I want to go with them," Rhoda pleaded.

"Why, you yellow cow. You're goin' where I say. To hell maybe, but you're goin' with me."

"That's my girl who said that," rendered Mrs. Purdue and again started moving forward.

"Please don't go any closer, Mrs. Purdue," pleaded Reverend Steele again. But the old woman continued until she stood only a foot or two in front of Lila and the gun.

"My own daughter shoot me, Reverend Steele?" She smiled weakly and shook her head. "Maybe she'd shoot her own father dead, but not her own mother. She would have her little sister do that job for her." Mrs. Purdue grimaced suddenly in complete pain. She doubled over slightly.

"You're hurt badly," shouted Buck. "Please come back here, Mrs. Purdue, or I'll have to come after you."

She straightened again. "Don't do that Sheriff Rhodes. Don't risk your life. She will not shoot me. And there may still be a chance to save my little Rhoda." She looked sadly to Rhoda. "You ain't all bad yet, Rhoda. You still got a chance. You got a lifetime ahead of you. Leave her now. She ain't no good. You still got a chance."

"Shut up you fool. She ain't leavin' cause she can't get outta' this neck lock. She stays right here."

"We try!" The old woman began and the tears flooded her pain-tired eyes. "We try so very hard to do it all so right. We try so hard. Maybe we can't do the things we'd like to do for our kids. Maybe we'd like to give them all the things in the world. But what do we do when we ain't got it to give them? And ain't got no way of getting it for them? But we try. We try ever so hard for them!" Then her eyes suddenly seemed to dry. They hardened noticeably and even Lila was taken back by the suddeness of the change. "We've talked long enough Lila. Rhoda, go up on the dock with the others."

"Another word outta' you, bitch-bat..."

"Don't waste your bullet. I ain't got much time

188

left." Then, softly for a brief instant, she looked to Rhoda again. "Under my bed is a package for you. A present. For your birthday tomorrow."

Rhoda cried unrestrainedly. "Ma! Ma! I'm sorry... so very sorry."

"Go to them, child, to your friends. Your real friends." And the old woman leaned forward to brush her cheek with a kiss. In the same move she lightly took Lila's arm from around her neck and pushed Rhoda behind her and toward the police beyond.

Lila levelled the gun. "Come back here! Come back or you're a dead broad!"

Mrs. Purdue used every ounce of strength she had left as she pushed Lila's arm upward and the gun fired harmlessly into the air. She at the same time pushed her backward and both, losing their footing, went over the guard rail and into the speeding propeller at the fan tail.

Jockey raced forward tearing at his shirt. "Somebody cut that motor quick!" He dove over the stern as the police and Reverend Steele raced in to board the ship. The little man's head came up for the first time just as the screw stopped its speeding revolutions, then he dove under again. After several minutes and many more dives, Chief reached over and pulled Jockey back aboard the ship. He looked to Reverend Steele who had his arm comfortingly around Rhoda's shoulders.

"Not a sign, Reverend. They're gone," he said slowly.

CHAPTER EIGHTEEN

Buck and Reverend Steele stood looking through the Sheriff's office window, across to the court-house as two of Buck's deputies brought Rhoda out and put her into the back seat of an awaiting squad car. One of the deputies got in beside her while the other took his place behind the steering wheel.

"She's got a long, rough, lonely day ahead of her," advanced Reverend Steele.

Buck picked up a paper cup from the water cooler as he walked back to his desk where he took out the half-bottle of whiskey. "Join me, Hank?"

Reverend Steele looked to him, shook his head, then turned back to look out through the window again.

The Sheriff glanced from the bottle to the paper cup, then crumpled the paper cup, let it fall into his waste basket and took a long pull at the bottle before he fastened the cap and replaced it in the desk. "Illicit narcotics breed a lonely life." He walked back to stand beside the clergyman at the window just as two hearses and several cars of a funeral procession passed. They watched intently as the squad car bearing Rhoda and the two deputies moved out from the curb and fell in immediately behind the last hearse.

"How do you say a service for a nice old lady and a rotten daughter, both at the same time, Hank?" Buck was serious.

Reverend Steele watched in silence until the last of the cars drove by. Then without turning he said strongly. "The Bible said it all for me, centuries ago… 'Tho' I walk in the shadow of death, I shall fear no evil'."

The two men walked out to the squad car which would take them along their street and to the cemetery at the edge of town.

—THE END—